Appraise Her

PAULA PRIAMOS

Cover Design and Interior Format

© THE KILLION GROUP INC.

For my late mother, Judy Burleson Priamos

CHAPTER ONE

THE WOMAN WITH whom I'd spent most of my morning is the third story on the evening news. She's behind the black smoke of a big rig explosion shutting down all northbound lanes of the 101 Freeway and a water main break on Sunset Boulevard. She is my new client, an old childhood friend, and she is missing.

Things don't quite add up.

How does one make it on the local news if gone for only a few short hours? She could've run out of gas and found her cell phone had lost its charge or signal for that matter. She could've just gone for a drive to clear her head and forgotten about the time.

Elise is not someone people would recognize, a losable face in the crowd, hard to spot in any convenience store surveillance tape, but that doesn't mean she's just anyone. She is the daughter of Hollywood royalty, the black and white Rat Pack kind, the reclusive Carson Davis, a legendary actor, eighty-one, three or four Oscars earned and countless nominations. A man who's never been caught in anything more casual than a golfing polo and trousers out on the green. The rest of the time he's been photographed either at dinner in a double-breasted suit or an awards event in a tux.

His handsome face fills the screen, upstaging his daughter even now when she is the subject the reporter is speaking about. Up until today when I met with his daughter to appraise some property, I too believed the reports that claimed he's been spending the last year or so retired in a whitewashed villa off the coast of Spain. Word of mouth and a home in Carson's name with high stucco walls to keep out paparazzi is all it took for the rumor to realize into truth.

But I saw with my own eyes.

The hospital bed. The ventilator. The body. The pump and hiss of air being forced into the motionless man's lungs is with me now, in my head, like the sounds of a large city or a noisy casino a day after you've left it. Spain was, at the very least, a lie.

From the family room I hear a pot skid on a burner in the kitchen and I smell the meal my fiancé is preparing the two of us for dinner. Something Italian with sausage, spices and tomatoes. Typically, on Monday nights, Hugh gets here after nine and we forgo this part of domestic life. We might go out for coffee at Starbucks or stay in and catch a movie before heading upstairs for sex and sleep. The rest of the work week he stays at his studio apartment in Santa Monica. As a contractor, with a complicated multi-level beach house that he's working on in Malibu, it only makes sense.

We will be each other's second marriage. Hugh is a widower. I'm a divorcee'. There's a difference of loss and failure between us. Even though we've been engaged for close to two months, I still can't bring myself to ask him to move in with me.

The reporter is saying something more about Elise. How a shoe has been found in the driveway of her home, a suede beige kitten heel she'd worn when she showed me around her father's mansion in Bel Air earlier today. Hardly enough evidence to call it an abduction. Some women choose to drive in their bare feet.

Yet it was proof enough to determine once she'd realized one shoe was gone why hadn't she come back for it? I'd complimented her on those two-inch heels, not because I'd wanted a pair for myself. I wanted to make a lasting impression. She might refer wealthy people she knew to me, people who frequently bought and sold property almost like a sport and who always needed an appraiser to help them turn a profit.

Elise and I had been childhood friends, but we'd lost touch with each other as far back as middle school. For a few years, before Carson decided to uproot his family to Malibu, they lived less than three blocks away in a neighborhood in Toluca Lake, an eclectic mix of middle-class families and wealthier ones, not far from the TV and movie studios. Instead of a three-bedroom custom built home like mine, the Davis Family lived in a much bigger spread with a wrought iron fence and swinging ten-foot gates.

As kids we'd been fierce competitors on the

tetherball courts, playing until the recess bell rang and the teacher threatened us with detention if we didn't come inside. I still have the calluses just under the surface of my palms. We were each other's first real challenge and maybe that was why she remembered me after all these years.

As adults we've reached out to each other now and then. She was in attendance for my first marriage, showing up briefly at the reception and generously gifting my new husband and me with a weekend stay at a five-star resort in Rancho Mirage, just outside of Palm Springs. I send her Christmas and birthday cards and she thanks me through friendly enough emails. We tenuously stay in each other's lives because there is a tie between us that cannot be broken nor can it be tended to very often.

Or maybe what she and I share runs deeper and has to do with how well she knows I can keep a secret, letting it become part of me like bone and blood. Maybe asking me to do the appraisal is a way of reminding me of that fact.

When I asked how she'd heard I was an appraiser she said it was through a friend of a friend, brushing it off as if I'd asked her something so trivial she'd never bother answering. And maybe she was right that it didn't matter. I get calls from real estate agents, loan workers from banks, and homeowners who find me in the yellow pages.

I'm about to head into the kitchen to tell Hugh about my personal connection to the woman who's just made the news. Hugh will listen intently, then call it a coincidence. I'm expecting to feel slightly deflated. Practical people take the energy out of any conversation.

"Dammit," I hear Hugh say.

At first, I think he's burned something, but there are muffled words after. He must be on his cell disputing something with his foreman about not enough sheetrock delivered or a permit that has not come through.

Possibly he could've lost the connection given the throng of trees that line either side of my property. Sometimes they block out the sun as well as the nearest cell phone tower which is why I still keep a landline number.

I decide to go outside and get the mail, the way I always do right before the sun is about to set. The metal box is a few yards from the porch. My small two-bedroom home is located in a quiet part of Laurel Canyon, off the curve of a narrow, paved road that turns into gravel and heads deep into thick live oak, shrubs and eucalyptus trees.

If I were to appraise my own home, it would sell for around 1.2 million. But I have no intentions of ever moving. Technically I'm in the woods yet not so far away from the city that I can't hear the traffic, commuters on the boulevard who use this steep cut-off to get from the Valley to West Hollywood.

In early fall, the air is cooler and the sky gets darker sooner yet it still feels like a shock. From the mailbox I pull out a couple of household bills, a postcard from my mother who refuses to learn about the conveniences of social media and post pictures of her travels online. This one is stamped in Vienna. My mother travels alone, though she doesn't usually stay that way for the duration of her trip.

She calls her male travel companions she picks up along the way "adventures." At sixty-five, she reasons, she is too old to be called a slut. The photo on the card is of an empty black gondola bobbing on green water.

She uses my full name Catia on the card because she finds it insulting how everyone lops off the first syllable and simply call me Tia. "Your name is beautifully Greek," she reminds me. "Like you. This nickname makes you sound like you should be in a bikini somewhere drenched in sun tan oil." Because of my background as a former handwriting expert, she must assume a picture of herself in front of a landmark would reveal very little.

I'm able to detect much more about her trip by reading her script instead of her smile. But it doesn't exactly work that way; there's more to it and besides, I'm really out of practice. I want to be out of practice. That has not been what I do as an occupation for some time. I'm an appraiser now.

On my way back to the house I spot what looks like the corner of a flyer left under the front door-mat. Another house painter looking for work or a teenager advertising yard work service. It wasn't here when I came home nearly an hour before. I pull out the flyer that is actually a sheet of white copy paper, folded in half. One line is written in black felt tip on the crease.

He's here early.

CHAPTER TWO

I DON'T TELL HUGH about the note. If I had it would've cut short the rest of our plans for the evening. Dinner would be put off while he took a look around outside, the fragrant red sauce simmering on the stove turned off, going cold and pasta sticking together as it drained dry in the colander.

A waste of time, of course. Whoever it was wouldn't be just lingering on my property, waiting to get caught.

Hugh is intimidating enough, at six feet tall, with dark blond hair, graying at the temples, and lean muscled arms. He is weathered strong like so many beach homes he either restores back to sturdy shape or builds from the concrete foundation to the vaulted wood beams and tile rooftops. He'd question me about who I thought would do such a thing. A neighbor with a crush? A creepy client? What about my ex-husband, Kyle?

No surprise that Hugh doesn't like Kyle. Most new fiancés don't like the former ex-husband, all that shared intimate history to compete with that only time, a deeper love and better, more emotionally connected sex will fade away.

A satisfying second marriage is a slow, hard-earned win.

My divorce from Kyle is only eleven months fresh. Sometimes I'm not sure if I'll ever fully get over what he and I lost because at times we'd been so happy. I could feel it off him too, when he held me close and repeated faintly like breath between us that I was his "Tia" as if my name alone meant more than any other words he could possibly come up with. We could be in a room full of people and it didn't matter. It was always just him and me. Call it a lapse in judgment, but it had been a contentment I didn't think twice about. There hadn't been another woman that broke us up. It had been a far bigger prospect of a person, a baby. Kyle doesn't want children and I do. Not children in the plural.

One child is all I'd asked for and we talked and talked about it until I finally grew too frustrated to continue. In the end, making a family was asking too much of my ex and his DNA.

Not quite touching forty, he's one of the youngest Associate History professors at UCLA. He's the type who prides himself on looking more like one of his students than part of the faculty. Kyle also moonlights as a real estate agent on the weekends. Saturdays are spent driving around LA in his leased brand new silver Mercedes Coupe, showing the kind of extravagant properties where the monthly mortgage alone is approximately his yearly professor's salary. His ability to seek out valuable properties and get them for a relatively rock-bottom price helped us snatch up the two-bedroom in Laurel Canyon before it hit the market, a fixer-upper, with a chunk of money I came into after I turned twenty-five and was given the portion of the life insurance policy my father left me in his will. Later, after a particularly sizeable commission came in, Kyle was able to buy another property, a condo in a high-rise near the ocean.

I should be grateful Kyle loves being around so much money. Agreeing not to take part of his real estate business in the divorce is what gave me the home in Laurel Canyon and half interest in the condo in Marina Del Rey.

My sister thinks I've made the kind of profound mistake I can't take back. Hugh is too old for me. To her, a man barely in his fifties somehow substitutes boxers with Depends and gulps down grainy glasses of Metamucil at every meal. It's all about the numbers with Laney. She's a mother of three young boys, her husband, a minor league baseball coach is her same age, thirty-eight. They live in a four-bedroom home in the suburbs of Portland, Oregon. Each of their children is roughly two years apart. "If only you'd just thought about it and stopped taking the pill," she'd recently said on the phone with me. "Women are expected to deceive their husbands when they're spooked about becoming fathers. Kyle would've learned to live with it. How do you think I got pregnant with Wyatt?" she asks me. "Dan wanted to stop at two. He loves them all. You've heard him. He balances the boys on his lap and calls them his Three Little Bench Warmers."

But Hugh doesn't need to be tricked. He already *enjoys* being a father to his eighteen-year-old daughter, a freshman at Washington State University in Seattle. Since his wife died nearly five years before, he's proven he can be enough of a parent to be the only parent.

If I'd shown Hugh the cryptic message I'd found on the front porch, he'd make me worry about something that is probably just a stupid prank. I wouldn't be lying in bed in the dark right after sex the way I always do now with my knees bent as he settles on to his side and snores slightly beside me. I wouldn't be lying here in this same position in the hopes that this time he and I are finally forming a connection in my womb. We've been trying for sixteen weeks, not enough time to suspect something is wrong with either of us but enough time to feel the possibility strengthen in my throat like a silent scream.

—◆—

The twin screw diesel yacht had six bedrooms, a large Jacuzzi on deck that could accommodate an entire cheerleading squad, a dining room that seated twelve and a half staircase that lead down to a lower level sitting room that overlooked the stern of the ship. A monstrous water craft easily worth nineteen million. And it was docked temporarily at a small wedge of a marina at Dana Point in Orange County.

The owner, a sixty-eight-year old oil tycoon celebrating the one-year anniversary to his fourth wife, was throwing one hell of a bash, a party that began mid-afternoon, only to pick up even more energy by dusk.

Trays of top shelf champagne and neatly crafted hors d'oeuvres sliders made with corn muffins and shredded barbecue beef were generously passed around, a skinned swine was cooked and impaled on a spit in the corner of the deck. A waiter dressed all in black stood nearby with a sharp blade to slice long pieces of flesh from the animal for hungry guests.

Everyone connected to the Texan mogul was invited, from members of the city council, to the mayor of Los Angeles who made a brief appearance and fellow business investors, bank workers, and me.

Over the last few years I'd appraised several homes for him in the LA area, raising the numbers, and, as a consequence, more than doubled his profits on several of them. Some appraisers didn't do enough groundwork. They assessed the home and the two or so near it.

But I did much more.

There were the dynamics of the affluent neighborhoods to consider, the low crime rates, and the fact that there were virtually no foreclosures in the immediate area to drive prices down. Many times, a wealthy neighbor would hear of an owner getting behind in payments and purchase the home outright just to avoid it going up for auction. I'd factor in years of market stability in my assessments.

By sunset the spacious luxury yacht became

more cramped with drunks. Most of the people I knew were clearing out. Even on the deck the smell of alcohol overpowered the salty ocean breeze. Girls that barely looked eighteen in string bikinis were climbing into the Jacuzzi. I spotted wife number four in a red thong, playfully splashing another woman's wet chest.

Things were about to get out of hand.

It was time for me to leave.

That was when Hugh approached me with his teenage daughter.

He was dark blond and attractive in a way that most men I came across weren't. If the deep-nicked wrinkles at the corners of his light blue eyes were any indication, he was a middle-aged man who'd spent his life showing his expressions, not keeping them in. His skin was tan, thickened from the sun, so I immediately pegged him as in construction even before he told me what he did for a living. But he cleaned up nicely, standing before me in a button down white shirt, jeans and charcoal gray sports jacket, ostrich cowboy boots. He had a man's build, unlike Kyle who never seemed to grow out of his boy's body.

Hugh introduced himself and his seventeen-year-old daughter Ashley, then apologized for approaching me in the first place.

The girls crowding into the Jacuzzi just a few feet away didn't turn him on. They alarmed him.

Would I mind staying with his daughter while he made the rounds and said his goodbyes? In the face of asking him why he'd bring his young daughter to such a party he was obviously upset by his own bad judgment. The party was quickly degrading into a rich man's fantasy.

Ashley looked nothing like her father, her eyes narrower than his, more focused on her surroundings, focused on me, and they were dark brown, not blue. When I asked her about where she planned on going to school she told me Washington State because her mother would want her to go there. It was her alma mater. She spoke of her mother in the past tense with a calmness I assumed was just a cover because the grief was still too fresh to share. The way she was acting along with her father having her tag along with him to a business gathering on a yacht made me think that her mother must've recently passed.

When Hugh returned he thanked me, then walked us both out to the parking lot, and while his daughter waited for him in the front seat of his truck, he handed me a business card. On the back he'd written another phone number along with the letter "H" either to abbreviate the first letter of his name or for the word home.

He didn't even try to get my number.

Instead he left it up to me and when I called the next evening we spoke for at least an hour. We talked on the phone every day for an entire week before we agreed to meet for dinner.

The business card with Hugh's writing on it I've since thrown out, but I remember the capital letter H, how large and neat it was, a perfectly block letter, how it overshadowed the numbers next to it that were much smaller in size.

I remember thinking it revealed he might be at

the worst deceitful or at best putting up a front of self-assurance. Not knowing which kept me from calling him that night. So the next day I wrote Hugh's number down again in my own hand, then threw out his business card.

Even though I'd stopped doing it as a job, reading people's handwriting had become as reflexive as a first impression. The truth was I was lonely and I liked him, this widower and father of a sad young daughter about to go off to college. And I wasn't going to allow the broad interpretations of one capital letter prevent me from seeing him again.

———◆———

Hugh is gone before daybreak, a construction site's most productive time being the morning hours before heat and hunger set in among the workers. A pot of coffee is brewed. Hugh is conscientious enough to bus his own mug and place it in the dish washer.

I pour myself a cup, in no rush. My morning is free. I'd planned on finishing up the paperwork on the Davis estate. The story on the news about Elise's disappearance is another thing I've kept from Hugh, though it hardly seems relevant when she most likely has already returned home by now.

It simply doesn't seem possible that something could've happened to her. I remember the confident man's handshake she'd given me when I arrived before suddenly moving to the delicate hug most women do when they see one another, as if it slipped her mind she was with an old friend. Everything, including my shock at seeing her father unable to breathe on his own, seemed to be under Elise's control yesterday.

Like the reporter had said, she had worn the tan suede pumps and a navy silk pantsuit with a plunging neckline to detract from the extra twenty pounds at her mid-section. If I'm honest, she looked old, a good ten to fifteen years more than myself, and I wonder if it's the secret knowledge of her father's fragile condition that has aged her so quickly. With the press teeming in aggressive packs along Robertson Boulevard and other celebrity hot spots not so many miles away from the estate, it certainly couldn't be easy to keep them off the scent of her ailing, immobile father.

In typical Elise-style, there had been no house-keeper or gardener on the grounds when I arrived at the Davis estate, though I am certain the family employs both. Possibly learning this maneuver from her screen icon of a father who's always safeguarded his private life, Elise, too, knows what it takes to keep prying eyes from seeing what she doesn't want them to see.

———◆———

Shortly after Elise's mother passed, I remember Carson in a dark mood, talking to a scrawny man with a nervous tick in his shoulders, a movie person, either an agent or an assistant, someone who was about to obediently follow orders. They were both in black suits, white shirts, black ties and a pink rose on the lapel, Elise's mother's favorite flower. The cut of Carson's suit hung perfectly while the man he was speaking to whose suit could have been just as expensive and well-tailored, next to Carson Davis just looked rumpled and cheap. A small group of us, my mother and me included, were at the house about to go to the closed casket viewing at the mortuary. Carson was persistent with my mother that I attend in order to provide his daughter a sense of comfort. No regard, on his behalf, for what the sight of confronting death in the form of another coffin might trigger in me at my young age, considering all that I'd recently been through. *I was fatherless.* In the past several months the brutal knowledge floated invisibly in front of me, behind me, trailing me everywhere. I couldn't get away from the pain. Elise's father wouldn't let up until my mother finally caved, the way most people did when it came to Carson convincing them of anything, and only agreed on the condition she went with me too.

"This is how you handle the media." Carson held up a fist to the scrawny guy. It was practically as big as a tough-skinned grapefruit, the hand with his wedding band on his ring finger. "You show them something flashy in this one," he said, before turning his wrist, showing the fist was empty. Then his middle finger shot up from the other hand, flipping off the guy who stood before him waiting on instructions for what Carson wanted him to do next.

Carson's smile that afternoon was not charismatic, it was dangerous.

I remembered Elise telling me her father grew up poor, in a cramped clapboard home that always reeked of cigarettes and boiled cabbage in South Boston. He was the only child of young alcoholic parents who couldn't stand one another and had trouble keeping the lights on and milk in the refrigerator. Sometimes Carson boxed bare fisted in the alleys with some of the older boys for a little extra cash - a coffee can they all contributed change and soft bills in, including some of the gruff male small owner merchants who'd once served as sailors or marines and now operated bars, laundromats and would pay top dollar to remember the rules-free street fights of their youth. They'd toss in five and ten dollar bills to make the pot worth a split lip, a finger permanently bent the wrong way, or an eye swollen shut for a week.

Carson may've lost the Massachusetts accent, but he didn't lose the tough talk of the neighborhood where he came from, nor did he lose the edge that outsmarted his opponents and always left him the last man standing.

The guy with Carson appeared stunned to be on the receiving end of such a rude gesture from one of the most powerful men in Hollywood who was no longer thinking like a celebrity, but only of his heartbroken family, his two young children who'd just lost their mother. "Then," Carson continued still referring to his middle finger, "they miss you're really doing this to all of them. You stupid sons of bitches just let the *big fucking story* get away."

Later I would learn while the paparazzi followed along behind our line of cars, taking the most obvious route from the Malibu house to the mortuary for the viewing, what Carson was really cheating them out of – hard proof in the form of Mrs. Davis's damning toxicology report. It was officially being replaced on file with a clean one, putting to rest the questions his wife was anything but sober at the time of the car accident that killed her and the innocent driver she hit head on.

◆

The forms I'd filled out yesterday of the Davis estate high up in the hills of Bel Air are in my bag and I pull them out. Among the ten thousand square feet of living space, the two granite fireplaces, the spiral handcrafted mahogany spiral staircase, chef's kitchen with marble countertops flown in from Italy, is the nine-foot-deep pool, a guest house and a half acre of green lawn. From there, the view extends beyond the rooftops of the residences beneath his, all the way to the tennis courts on the UCLA campus. Easily the property is worth thirty million.

I'm not lawfully supposed to be an advocate for any client.

No predetermined value set on a property, not even a hint to the seller. But is that the silent agreement made when Elise hired me instead of someone she already had worked with? She did not necessarily live off her father's money.

She'd made more with the money he'd given her on her thirtieth birthday five years before. In less than eighteen months she'd doubled her trust by investing in a software startup company with two twenty-year-old computer geeks as well as becoming a partner in a set of indoor shopping malls in the Midwest that touted a working water park twelve months out of the year. "Who doesn't want to have their wet hair smell of chlorine and order an ice cream cone in a bathing suit in sub-zero temperatures?"

Elise had said this right when we were still chatting in the foyer, before I headed upstairs, before I saw what I did and thought differently of her.

Was she really so cold as to sell her father's home literally right out from under his hospital bed? Was the pressure of what she was about to do too much? Is that why she was missing; she needed to rethink things?

How easily it could've been for Elise to keep me from seeing her father, the eerie stillness of his body beneath the thin woven blanket and crisp white sheet. His eyes were closed, but with the tube from the ventilator taped to his mouth he hardly appeared at peace. Technically appraisers don't have to see and take pictures of every single room, especially a home of such a grand scale.

I'd been ahead of Elise on the staircase. A technical question about the appraisal process could've stopped me on those steps and bought her time. Not far from the top of the staircase the door to Carson's room had been left open.

A woman with short dark hair was seated in a chair near the bed, a hardback spread spine-up across her lap. She'd looked up at me with an expression of casual disinterest, before returning to what she'd been reading. No nurse's uniform, the woman was in a sweater and expensive dress pants I guessed had to be dry-cleaned. A private doctor?

"I'm sorry," I stumbled, "I didn't know."

The woman remained quietly reading as if I'd already gone away.

Elise touched my shoulder, guiding me deeper down the hallway. She would be doing all the talking.

"Most don't, Catia," she'd said using my real name.

Unlike my mother, it wasn't because Elise felt my nickname "Tia" didn't suit me. It was because *she* liked the sound of my birth name off her tongue.

"But I think, *I know*, I can trust you not to betray me or my father by telling anyone about the change in his medical condition."

"A change" Elise had said like she was breezily referring to a change of scenery, not the difference between being conscious and in a coma.

My cell phone vibrates on the kitchen table. After my trip to the Davis estate I'd neglected to turn the ringer back on. I have three recent calls and two messages. One is a hang-up, the next is from my ex-husband reminding me I'm supposed to meet him later this afternoon and the last call, the one I've just missed, is from a detective. He wants to speak with me about Elise. His voice sounds professional, also a little irritated that I hadn't picked up and he could finish with me in one phone call.

Maybe I'd been wrong about Elise.

I see her struggle with her assailant, the fear in her eyes at being ambushed in her own driveway, a place where she naturally let her guard down, a place where she felt safe. She's dragged from behind, kicking out to free herself, losing a shoe as she's forced back into her car and driven to some drastic end.

My name has come up to trace her last hours.

The last thing I want is to be part of another investigation. With the flurried advancements of technology, people rarely put much down on paper. Except for our signatures, we've become a virtual stranger to our own hand. It's one of the reasons why I chose another line of work.

There is no intimacy of the written word anymore. Thoughts and to-do lists are stored in smart phones or iPads. Most people rely on an electronic book with a screen that fakes a type written page of a paperback or hardback rather than carry around the real thing with pages that still smell of the printing. Directions are fed into a computer built into every new car and spoken back to the driver using a mechanical female voice.

But if pressed I could assess whether someone is egotistical or shy or holding something back just by taking a look at something as inconsequential as their grocery list. And I still spot people clutching those, wandering down the bread or produce aisle of a store with a scrap of paper filled with their messy, revealing words.

I once accurately predicted a young fifteen-year-old Japanese boy had falsely confessed to killing his own mother in the kitchen of their home. She was brutally struck several times in the temple with an object that was square and solid as a brick but had never been recovered. The boy's words, as I studied them, *"I hit her with something hard"* were spaced far apart like he'd needed time to think of his lie. The emphasis on certain words like "bled out so much" and "her eyes wouldn't shut," phrases that were much darker in lead pencil than the rest of his confession made it clear to me he was just as traumatized as he was scared. He'd seen who had left his mother in a pool of her own blood on the kitchen linoleum.

Through several meetings with a court appointed counselor it was later determined the boy was petrified of his stepfather, a cruel man who repeatedly abused both his wife and her son, blackening eyes, breaking bones. Because the boy feared no one would believe him if he pointed the finger at the right person, he would prefer a life behind bars to living with his mother's murderer.

I call the detective back on my cell while weaving in and out of college students on the UCLA campus. It's a sunny afternoon, still warm enough in early October for shorts and t-shirts. Most of the students I pass are walking slow, humped over, texting on their phones. Kyle wants to meet at Kerckhoff's Coffeehouse, his convenience, not mine, but somewhere I nevertheless agreed to.

"You've reached Detective Antonio Ramirez," the message starts. He's a tired sounding man no matter how professional he tries to come off, probably at the job longer than he should be.

I wait for the beep and give him information he already has, my name and number. I, too, want to get this conversation over with. I can't provide much information on Elise except for maybe spilling the fact her father lay in the last stage before death upstairs in his home in Bel Air. Would the media be camped at the Davis estate by now? Would the empty house in Spain be swarmed too? Had Elise's secret already been found out?

The coffeehouse is on the second floor of Kerckhoff Hall and has a glass display case of sugary fruit pastries and a menu of deli sandwiches stacked high with lunch meats.

Kyle is seated at a table in the front by a window, reading a book as thick as the Bible. The cover is visible, a black and white photo of an older man with wire rimmed glasses, standing at a podium, his mouth open in mid-speech. It's about former President Harry Truman, a scholarly biography Kyle has probably read before but is doing again to keep his knowledge intact. He doesn't like to slip-up during his lectures. He prides himself on instantly supplying, as if by natural reflex, the right answers to a student's questions.

He's in the common casual professor's look of a long sleeve button down, tucked into jeans, and he's let his hair grow longer, a more youthful look to go with his new twenty-something girlfriend, a graduate student named Becca.

Not Rebecca. Becca. Apparently, she's even dropped her last name because it gives her bad memories. Becca likes to be in relationships with both men and women and her last entanglement before Kyle was with a woman who clearly left her in knots.

Things only straightened out once her former lover got a restraining order out on Becca, something that was none of my business yet my ex-husband informed me of anyway. "Passion got the better of her," he explained. "Most break-ups don't end as reasonably as ours." Clearly that had been a slight at me. That I didn't go crazy when he walked out or had I kicked him out? Either way, it hadn't mattered. He still left. Mourning the loss of our marriage through crushing sadness, tears and sleepless nights doesn't cut it for my ex-husband. I was supposed to slit open the crotches of his four tailored suits, then slice across the veins on the whites of my wrists and call him, begging for a second chance as I slipped into a lukewarm bath. The fact is, Kyle has sought out the kind of chaos and drama in his life that a bright, seemingly imbalanced, yet probably seductive younger woman can give him.

As I stand across the room from him, it hits me again, the force of it so strong I feel like I might fall over.

My ex-husband has found somebody else.

He doesn't want me.

Kyle raises a full palm to me, a slight smile. His other hand is holding onto a spoonful of chili. As I reach the table, I see he's ordered me a toasted club sandwich, something he must know I won't eat and he can take it in a to-go container to have later. This isn't a lunch date. I don't plan to stay very long.

"You look good, Tia," he says.

I'm in a jean skirt, sandals and a navy t-shirt and my light brown hair is still in a wavy bob that Kyle used to like on me. He said it showed off my best feature, my green eyes, not as rare of a feature for Greeks as some might think. But I haven't kept the hairstyle for him. It's something I like too.

His compliment shouldn't do something inside me but it does. In time I remind myself again, this man who broke my heart will have no physical effect on me. For now, though, a part of me hates that I'm still flattered he notices me in that way.

I'm not one of those embittered people who had to sell off the matrimonial bed or his prized juicer that he made fresh orange juice with every morning or the dinner table and chairs where we sat and talked, we laughed and, towards the end, we stubbornly remained silent. I wrote him a fair check for his share of the furnishings. The juicer was one of the first things I sent him once he settled into his new apartment in West Hollywood. The pulp used to get stuck in my front teeth anyway.

I'm hoping Kyle isn't fishing for a compliment about his long rock star bangs. "Thanks. So what do you need to tell me?"

"It's about our condo at the marina."

"You could've told me over the phone. Unless," I add, "that it's burned down."

Kyle chuckles. A cute couple in workout clothes call out to him from line. The girl looks like she's just come from yoga and the guy from a sweaty run.

"Hey, Professor Wilkins."

Kyle looks over at them and holds up the peace sign.

I roll my eyes. I imagine he probably gets stoned on the weekends with his students and shows off his historical trivia, about the sixties, Woodstock and free love. I'm sure he exaggerates about how much money he makes as a part-time real estate agent to the rich.

My ex-husband has always tried too hard to be liked. Some might find this charming while I see it as a shortcoming.

"I think we should hold off on listing it."

"But we agreed…"

"I know, Tia," he says. "But you know as well as anyone the market is down right now."

A female employee is clearing the dirty plates off a nearby table and I get her attention, mouthing the words "to-go box, please." Suddenly I'm hungry and I'm not about to leave here empty handed. I'm taking this huge sandwich Kyle doesn't think I'll eat home with me. Maybe I'll toss the contents on the side of the road close to home and let the coyotes feast on it.

I face him.

"The market is actually stabilizing."

Kyle reaches across the table for me, but I lean back. He settles the flat of his hand on the space in the middle next to the salt, pepper and red pepper shakers.

For the nearly ten years we were married it was Kyle's way to rush me, even bully me into making decisions that benefited him too, like when he pressured me into buying a boxy pre-owned Prius because one of us had to look environmentally friendly or the last time when he heartlessly tried to talk me out of wanting a baby.

"Listen, let's make a few renovations on the place. New carpeting in the two bedrooms, a fresh coat of paint on the walls. Switch out the kitchen linoleum and front room with hardwood. We could list it by next summer and double our profit."

This relatively small fifteen hundred square feet of coveted property by the water is the last tie he and I have with each other. In the divorce papers we stipulated we'd sell it as soon as possible. Now it seems Kyle is dragging his feet.

"Is there a reason why you need the extra money?" I have to ask. While he's always known how to pick a real estate bargain, Kyle also knows how to overextend himself, living a three-hundred-dollars-a-bottle-of-wine-for-dinner life that surpasses the salary of a college professor. Commissions from his sales can be few and far between in the market he works in where a potential client's credit gets checked before he even agrees to meet and show that person any properties so he doesn't waste his time. I imagine the new young girlfriend wants to be entertained and has him zeroing out his bank account every month, racking up his credit cards.

Kyle looks uncomfortable like I've hit a nerve.

"Nothing I can't handle. I have a couple of opportunities about to pan out."

"Well, Hugh and I have plans next summer."

"I get it," Kyle interrupts. "You've set a date."

It's the first sign of agitation he's shown me since before the divorce. In our Los Angeles real estate circle, we sometimes run into each other, and so far, we've always remained kiss-on-the-cheek civil. That's how I found out about Becca. He wanted me to hear it from him first.

"That's practically a year away, Tia. How long have you been seeing him, five, six months?"

I don't like what he's getting at.

"Ten," I correct him. "Engaged for eight of them."

But even as I say it, I realize Kyle is openly suggesting Hugh is my rebound which he most definitely is not. I will myself not to take the bait.

"You're saying Hugh and I won't make it till then?"

Kyles shakes his head. Secretly he's pleased with himself for making me sound defensive which is not the same as confident and he knows it.

"It takes a while to get to know someone, that's all."

"Thanks for the lecture, Professor Wilkins."

The employee returns with my to-go container, a signal Kyle is running out of time.

"Just think about it, Tia. I'll call you in a couple days."

I'm not sure if he's referring to what he's said about Hugh or the condo.

A young woman in a button down shirt dress, a wide belt, and slip on tennis shoes zeroes in on us from across the room.

There is no doubt her focus is on me.

Her hazel eyes are practically yellow under the light. She's carrying a canvas book bag. The buttons of her dress are undone enough for me to see the plastic front clasp of her lace bra, the pushed-up mounds of her breasts. This must be Becca. Her peroxide hair is frizzy, evenly parted right down the middle. Bright red lipstick and fake eyelashes, she is not the natural beauty I'd pictured, more like a woman dressed in a bad disguise. She is no fresh-faced young college student, though she is, in her own way, alluring, a nearly complete puzzle with a couple of key pieces missing.

I imagine she's closer to thirty than twenty-five. I don't see how my ex-husband doesn't see it too.

From behind Kyle, she puts both hands firmly on his shoulders. He doesn't flinch at her touch. Obviously, this isn't the first time she's sneaked up on him. Her forearms are covered in matching black and purple paisley patterned tattoos, her clipped nails are painted a cloudy white.

"I thought you'd be done with your ex by now," she says.

What she's suggesting hangs in the air. Rude, yes, but not entirely inaccurate.

"I thought so too," I answer as I get up to leave.

Let Kyle talk his way out of inviting me to lunch to his new girlfriend who already sounds unhinged enough to have a protective order filed against her. Had he told her he'd be here with me and she's just gotten out of class and decided to drop by or has she been watching us this whole time? I think of the note left on my doorstep the day before.

He's here early.

Before leaving the two of them at the table, I glance down at Becca's book bag curious if she's in possession of a black felt tip pen.

CHAPTER THREE

IN BED THAT NIGHT I'm watching the eleven o'clock news, my hand on the flat of my stomach. It feels no different than twenty-four hours before when Hugh pulled out from inside me. Another month living with a barren womb. Naturally I won't know if I'm pregnant for a couple weeks. Doesn't a woman sense when she's just had successful baby-making sex? Isn't that why so many women who don't want babies flock in fear to the drug store for the morning after pill?

If Hugh had come over tonight, we'd be able to double our chances during the time I'm ovulating. But I don't want my fiancé to feel he's nothing but a sperm donor. At thirty-five he says I have plenty of time, which I know I don't. I have *some time.* By my age conceiving will prove harder. It would be easier if I just ask Hugh to move in with me.

All he has is a copy of the house key to come and go as he pleases. Yet he always calls first. I'm still somehow making him feel like a visitor in a place that will be his home too come next summer. I still have so much to plan. Only the venue has been booked, a set of cabins in the

San Bernardino Mountains with lace curtains and a courtyard in between where we'll strewn white lights. Flowers, catering, the music and my wedding dress, all the details most brides enjoy pouring over, still have to be figured out.

The empty to-go container lays opened on the bed covers. I'd eaten the sandwich Kyle ordered for me for lunch as a late dinner in bed. When Hugh isn't here cooking for me I eat like I'm still in college. Take-out, some crackers and cheese, a bowl of cornflakes.

Elise's disappearance takes up a good portion of the newscast. So far over a hundred or more tips have been called in that police are following up on. There have been no sightings of her or her charcoal gray BMW SUV. Suddenly the screen fills with Breaking News, a statement from Elise's family has just come in.

I'm deeply concerned about the whereabouts of my daughter, Elise. However, the police are doing an incredible job keeping me informed of the investigation and I'm wholly confident Elise will be brought home safe and sound.
~Carson Davis

I use the remote to press pause.

It doesn't read *The Davis Family.* It reads *Carson Davis.* Who believed these were Carson's actual words? The man has a plastic tube taking up his throat. In his condition he can't speak, nor can he write or communicate with anyone. The man is unconscious, a true movie star even on his deathbed, wearing a pair of tan silk pajamas, his wavy white hair carefully combed and a hopeful gold crucifix hanging from his neck, which I find a little odd. I remember Elise coming to my house to help decorate the tree because her father didn't believe in Christmas.

Which family member issued this statement to the media?

I'm not even sure who is part of the Carson Davis Family. Carson's parents died years before on the east coast, one from cirrhosis of the liver, the other in a convalescent home Carson paid for yet never visited. Elise has an older brother, Edward, whom I hardly know except for one memorably embarrassing encounter. Mostly I've seen pictures of him scattered throughout the house. Having inherited his father's iron jaw line, he held the possibility of one day being as attractive as his father. He'd spent most of his time at a preppy Maryland boarding school when she and I were kids.

Maybe he is responsible for the statement to the media.

Their mother died decades before in that violent head on collision on Pacific Coast Highway when Elise was just thirteen, the year after I lost my father. The headlines left out Mrs. Davis's blood alcohol level or what had driven her that afternoon to get behind the wheel so heavily intoxicated. They left it out because Carson robbed them of those facts. He was with his lover at the time of the accident, a vocal coach who helped him carry a tune in his first musical. He won an Oscar for that role and once he suddenly became a widower he soon made her his second wife. After the acclaim started to ebb so did his affections for the vocal coach because he divorced her within the year.

Jordan is now on screen. His face is fuller, his hair thinner, just another thirty-something guy aging badly behind a work desk. Only he's been Assistant District Attorney of Los Angeles County for a while, soon running for mayor in the next election.

Any chance to show himself in the media, he takes it.

He's promising the viewers that the city's police force will track down Elise's whereabouts and if foul play is involved, there will be severe repercussions.

For many I'm sure he sounds sincere.

I was sincere the lifetime ago when I told him I loved him.

Although this isn't the first time I've seen him on TV, I change the channel, choosing to fall asleep to a mixture of light and motion on the screen instead of turning everything dark.

CHAPTER FOUR

~Back Then~

*M*OST OF MY *college friends smoked weed, the reek of an unwanted secondhand high seeping into my clothes, my lungs, just by hanging out with them. Back then romantic long-term relationships didn't count for much and acts of promiscuity which pretty much occurred every weekend on campus were blamed on a mind blurry from drugs and alcohol. "Oh my God, I shouldn't have blown him, but I had soooo much of that keg last night."*

One morning I walked in on one of my girlfriends naked, straddling some random male in her dorm room. Her official boyfriend was a basketball player at an away game in Oregon. Her bed was so squat that one of her feet in a cute white ankle sock was touching the floor. She and I had plans to go jogging on the track. It was our first year at California State University, Long Beach and I enjoyed running laps outside, breathing in all that clean-smelling ocean air.

All I saw of the guy was his bare feet and hairy legs. His hands were absent from touching her hips or her back.

He groaned. "Fuck, Jessica. I'm close."

My friend didn't stop moving on him even though

she turned her head and noticed me standing in the doorway. She didn't try and cover up her shame with a sheet. Neither of them had thought to lock the door. Behind me were the loud sounds of the active hallway, girls going to and from the bathroom showers with their plastic caddies and bath towels in hand. My dorm room was three doors away. There was the risk of someone else we knew popping their head in to say hi. My chest burned at the thought of someone catching me just standing there watching the two of them go at it like some kind of voyeur. I'd have to change schools.

My friend leaned towards the guy she was on top of.

"Could you wait for me downstairs, Tia?"

I nodded, quickly left, the thud of the heavy door closing as I reached the staircase to the lower floor. Outside, I waited, stretching my legs by the bicycle racks. Part of me fought the urge to head for the track by myself.

But I didn't want to lose Jessica as a friend. I hadn't made that many of them yet. The other girls on the floor might laugh and question why I'd get so worked up over seeing Jessica screwing some boy.

It was nothing. He was nothing. She had a real boyfriend, remember?

Minutes later, when the two of them came down fully dressed, I recognized him from our Political Science general ed class. He had long dirty blond hair and traveled the campus on a worn out skateboard. His parents were wealthy lawyers that lived in Hancock Park.

He and Jessica were talking a good foot apart, suddenly needing their space. They could've been discussing class notes. The intimacy was now over.

Next came the goodbye hug and while he had my friend in his arms, her face against his chest, I saw his attention was now on me, the girl who must've still appeared positively spooked at what she'd just witnessed. I remembered his first name was Jordan. Something about me sparked his interest. Later, after he and I started steadily dating, publicly being seen hand-in-hand at parties or in between classes, he would tell me he knew what that look on my face meant that morning. I had to be a virgin.

CHAPTER FIVE

MY JOB THE next day is assessing a set of duplexes on the wrong side of Wilshire Boulevard in Beverly Hills. This is considered the poorer part of the city where the value of properties plummet separated by a few hundred yards of asphalt. I decide to leave early and stop off at Elise's home in nearby Brentwood beforehand.

The victim's home is sometimes the meeting place between family and the authorities working the case. It also could be considered the crime scene. Elise's disappearance is looking more and more like a kidnapping. If so, when I get there her home will most likely be filled with police.

I was hired once by the distraught parents of a kidnapped eighteen-year-old girl to decipher the ransom note requesting five hundred thousand dollars. An entire bloody thumbnail, a gruesome bargaining chip, was sent along with it. The father was the head of a marketing firm in Orange County, the mother a stay-at-home mom. I compared the handwriting of all the family members and the seventy-five employees, and I found a match. The note was written by the teenage kidnap victim herself. Turned out she was an impulsive, spoiled girl so furious that her parents wouldn't fund the summer trip she wanted to take with friends after graduation all throughout Europe that she tore off her own nail with needle nose pliers.

Did Elise somehow sense she was in danger? Is that the real reason why she contacted me, someone with whom she easily could've found out has a previous relationship working with the police?

Most childhood friends are long since forgotten, yet all these years later Elise searched me out. For better or worse, she knew she could trust me. It's why she let me go ahead of her on the stairs at her father's home. She needed to show me the quiet trauma of an icon on his deathbed that was being kept from the rest of the world. Now that she's missing hours after meeting with me, I can't just let it go.

Once I'm at Elise's address, it is oddly quiet. No real police presence except for a private security guard parked a couple houses down, the driver still inside, behind the wheel. A forensics technology expert should be here searching through her home computer, others on the force combing through her desk, even the notes left under a magnet on her fridge door. Any signs of someone she intended to meet. Elise's landline must already be tapped in case there's a ransom call.

A newer shiny black Audi sedan is parked in her driveway, in the same spot where Elise was taken. The address of her residence is not on the appraisal forms I've finished filling out but the business card she gave me. Like me, she works out of an office at her home.

She lives in Brentwood, an upscale neighborhood where most of the properties are comfortably spaced out and protected by stucco walls, wrought iron gates and security cameras pointed at the entrance to the driveway.

Elise's home is not one of them. Her two-story white colonial with black shutters is wide open to the street.

The person who attacked her could've easily waited until she pulled into the drive, then came up on her from behind. There would virtually be no witnesses considering the neighboring homes on either side of hers are shrouded with six- foot high manicured bushes.

The more money one has the more one gets to isolate.

In front of Elise's home are overhanging oak trees, the roots pushing up cracks in the sidewalk. A white Escalade sits in the circular driveway across the street, an older style Mustang in mint condition with out of state plates is parked curbside in front of the house next door.

Halfway down the block a local channel news van lies in wait. Clearly limitations have been set with how close the media can get to Elise's home. Even though the crime happened *right here,* most reporters are obviously drawn to the celebrity aspect of the story, camped out twenty minutes away at the gates of Carson's eight figure estate. Because they don't know any better, they'll be anxiously waiting to film a glimpse of the man who will never come walking upright out the front door in his signature double-breasted suit or golfing attire again.

The official statement released to the press made it sound as if Carson was not only fully aware but keeping tabs on what was going on in regards to his daughter's disappearance. The press must eagerly be assuming he is either en route back to the States from his villa in Spain or already slipped into his mansion sometime overnight.

When I get out of my car I hold up the appraisal forms to show the guard who's just noticed me that I'm all business. He tips his Starbucks coffee cup in response, giving me the go ahead.

The walkway is made of brick with tidy pruned rosebushes lining either side. Through the front window a Persian cat flicks its tail on the sill. Elise struck me as a dog person, a big bouncy golden retriever or Labrador she'd happily trip over.

I ring the bell. When I don't get an answer, I also knock. At least one member of Elise's family must be inside or else the security guard in his car would've most likely stopped me from coming to the front door.

There's the sense that I'm being watched, so I glance back towards the window. A woman is staring at me, stock still, as if she is quiet enough I'll think no one is home. Instantly she and I recognize one another. If she is thinking of waiting for me to go, it is now too late. I've seen her and have no plans on leaving. Several seconds later, longer than it should take, the front door opens.

Standing before me is the short-haired woman

who'd been at Carson's bedside the other day. She has on a pinstriped oxford shirt tucked into black pants. Her lips are outlined in red liner yet not filled in like she'd forgotten or it had worn off. In her hand is a glass tumbler of vodka and orange juice on ice. Unlike a dog who wags its tail or barks at every stranger, the cat from the windowsill snakes in between her legs, then trots off into another room, ignoring me completely.

"I'm Catia," I say, adding, "Elise's friend from the other day. Is any of her family here?"

"*I'm* Elise's family." The woman extends her free hand, softening her approach after correcting me. "Deborah, Elise's wife."

I'm startled by the sound of a car starting behind me on the street, the sudden burst of loud music turned down by the driver, the deep rumbling sound of the engine like that of the classic Mustang I'd just seen parked in front of the neighbor's house.

Deborah appears annoyed by the noise as she takes a step back and shows me into the living room. The nude nylons she has on make scratching sounds on the carpet. The furniture in the living room is tasteful, dark wood and blush colored fabric on the couch, two matching floral print high-backed arm chairs.

I take a seat on the couch and Deborah sits down on the next cushion, intentionally crowding me, the pressure already on that I shouldn't outstay my welcome.

"Elise is a very private person. We've been married nearly a year. Not many people know."

We no longer live in a society that is so condemning of gay marriage. The reason why the two of them kept their relationship a secret doesn't make much sense.

"When I saw you sitting with her father I thought you were a doctor or some kind of care giver."

Deborah nods. This would be the right time for her to fill in the rest, the concocted story of him basking in a villa in Spain, why she was at Carson's estate in Bel Air watching over him on the ventilator machine, but she doesn't. She is remarkably put together for a woman whose spouse is missing. However, I couldn't picture Elise with a person who falls apart in times of crisis either.

"I am," she finally says. "A neurologist, though I research and publish articles in medical journals more than I treat patients these days." She stops as if she's told me enough. There's a tinge of regret in her voice as if she might've given up her practice to help take care of Carson.

Deborah points at the papers in my hand.

"Is that the appraisal for the estate?"

"Yes, but I really should…"

She takes the forms so fluidly it's as if I handed them to her.

"Thank you," she interrupts. "I'll give these to our attorney."

I hadn't planned on giving my appraisal to this woman. The forms had merely been my excuse to get into Elise's home.

"On the news last night, I saw the supposed

statement by Carson."

Deborah picks up on my tone, though doesn't appear too worried. That's when it occurs to me that Carson and all that medical equipment keeping him alive have probably already been removed from the estate.

Where might've Deborah taken him? To a convalescent home? A hospital? There was a reason the family put out that statement to the press and it was to deceive the public into thinking Carson was in full control of his faculties, to ensure some much-needed time. Deborah must've known as soon as the press caught wind of Elise's disappearance they'd swarm Carson's estate and then there would be no moving him without him being seen for what he is now – a body with nerve endings, but no brain activity, connected to this life by artificial means.

"Have the police contacted you?" she asks me.

"Yes, a detective left a message. I haven't had a chance to speak with him yet."

"Catia, I'm sure Elise wouldn't mind me sharing with you that her father's divorce with his third wife is nearly finalized. What a mistake he made with that one."

Deborah takes a sip of her drink.

"A greedy young flight attendant he brought home from a trip to Kauai. They've been separated for a while. There's a prenup, of course. But still, if she knew about his poor health she might draw things out in the courts."

Deborah studies my face to see if I'm being moved at all by her words. As a doctor I doubt many people can read her. She restrains her feelings for a living and thinks in detached, clinical terms – diagnoses and forms of treatment.

"They might put a freeze on all his accounts. Elise co-manages a foundation with children suffering from heart diseases in Carson's name."

"Do they have any children?"

"No, thank God."

"Elise has a brother," I say. For a moment I try and imagine what he looks like today, that fifteen-year old boy I'll never forget being alone in a dark kitchen pantry with. *Your brother-in-law* I want to add because she's made no mention of him yet and he was as close to Elise growing up as her wife must think she is to her now.

"He's in Nepal, charity work of some sort. I'm trying to get word to him about her."

"Has there been any news?" I ask.

We both know I'm referring to the investigation into Elise's disappearance.

Deborah sets her glass down harder on the coffee table than I imagined she meant it to.

"A few leads. They're going to conduct a search tomorrow, an area in the Hollywood Hills. It's been less than forty-eight hours and they're already looking for *her body*."

She looks away with disgust, grief rising to the surface in her eyes.

"They give up on the living so goddamn easily."

"What about you?"

Her eyes are on me again, narrowing at my question because it's about her.

"What do you mean?"

"Do you have anyone who can be with you while the police continue investigating?"

"I've asked everyone to leave. I'm not completely alone."

She touches the waistband of her pants and I see I'm dead wrong about the alcohol. It really is just a short glass tumbler of ice cubes and orange juice.

Kyle used to joke that I was an expert at understanding the motives behind people's handwritten words, but I was slow when it came to reading their body language.

"I'm about to start my second trimester," Elise says.

I shouldn't be jealous of a woman whose spouse is most likely dead, but I am. I am jealous of the inner joy growing inside her, building into tissue, the watery sounds of a faint heartbeat, translucent toes and fingers on her next sonogram. There will be grief to experience if Elise's lifeless body is recovered in the brush of the Hollywood Hills or somewhere else. The promise of a new life will carry Deborah on.

Glen, the real estate agent listing my next appraisal, is waiting with his female protégée who is in a drab pantsuit, a shock of hot pink camisole underneath and stilettos. No doubt he's bedding this girl or I think at least instructing her on how to dress to get him all worked up.

He looks at me like I'm ten minutes late when in actuality I'm early by five. Everyone is on

Glen's time.

At six feet tall, he has a swipe of graying brown hair at the top of his nearly bald head and a bit of a belly that no amount of marathons he runs throughout the year seems to ever shed. His narcissism, customized sports car and predilection for young women would make him the perfect drinking buddy for Kyle, if they could stand being in the same room together. Kyle sees all the ugly flaws in Glen's character yet notices none of them in himself.

Before Glen has a chance to come over and greet me, I take a fast snapshot of the exterior stucco and tile rooftop of the small six unit set of duplexes. I take another picture of the stiff artificial grass, a touch of added value to the property since California is a state so often in a drought.

Glen gives me the once over, shaking my hand a little longer than he should. His breath smells of the meaty lunch he must've just eaten. A mixed-up rumor started about Glen that he served six months in prison back East for a white-collar crime before he settled here in L.A., something about bilking wealthy older women out of their dead husband's retirement money or embezzling from the firm he once worked for as a stock broker. As typical of our social circle, nobody bothered to confirm either rumor. It is easier to spread the word not to trust him and speak badly of him behind his back.

"You and I need to work together more often," he says. "I like a lady who shows up on time."

Across the narrow courtyard that could be

used for sunbathing or barbecues, Glen trails me. Somewhere along the way, his female protégée has fallen behind which makes me wonder if this is intentional on her part.

For the next fifteen minutes as I inspect the six-car carport and the interior of the property, I'm conscious of walking in front of Glen in a cream-colored pencil skirt, boots, a black linen blouse tucked in. Men like Glen don't recognize, they don't care, how uncomfortable they make a woman feel. The predatory nature of the scene they set alone is its own form of sexual charge.

Once inside a second story apartment, I'm grateful for all the open space, at least seven hundred feet of polished hardwood floor. The room is empty, filled with afternoon sunlight until the length of Glen's shadow overtakes mine.

As I move into the kitchen, I act like I'm simply focusing on finishing my assessment instead of trying to get the hell away from him. New improvements must be included in my appraisal like a black granite countertop in the kitchen and the two glass shelves in the large rectangular window to grow plants or fresh herbs.

"So out with it, Tia." Glen is too close again. Maybe I am pregnant because his rancid slaughter house breath suddenly makes me feel nauseous. I hate that someone has told him my nickname, and he sounds like he's some sort of a friend. He and I rarely work together.

After today I'd like to keep it that way, but being on the favorites list with banks and real estate agents isn't easy. I've worked hard to be on it. All it would take to get my name removed is for Glen to lie and say I underestimated the worth of this property. I need the steady income.

Glen taps the toe of his dress shoe on the kitchen floor.

"How much is this set of shacks going for?"

"Three and a half," I say. "Maybe three point six."

He appears satisfied with the value I've come up with. We both know I'm giving him an added one hundred-thousand-dollar bone.

"Hugh tells me he's taken *you* off the market."

The comment is supposed to be a joke, a little bad real estate humor. All it sounds is sexist.

"How do you know Hugh?"

When Glen smiles I notice he has a mouth full of tall horse teeth. His eyes fixate on the second open button of my blouse like he'd like to bite it off, the third and the fourth too until my blouse is completely ripped open.

If I step back, he might get more aggressive and I'll find myself against the wall. If I stand my ground, which I'm not always good at, he might realize he won't be getting anywhere with me. *Where is his assistant in the unflattering pantsuit and hooker heels?*

"We go way back," Glen says. "My wife used to be friends with Carolyn, you know, his late wife. I'm sure he's told you about her."

I nod, though Hugh hasn't said much about Carolyn other than she was a good wife and an even better mother to their daughter and she tragically died too soon. I've never held that against him. Most men try their best not to talk to their new fiancée about their former wife, especially if it's their late wife whom they'll always love. As a consequence, there's a part of Hugh's heart I'll never have.

"I've listed quite a few homes he's renovated over the years," Glen goes on.

It's startling to hear that Glen, a chronic womanizer, actually has a wife waiting for him at home. Equally startling is trying to imagine my generous, good-hearted fiancé out on a double date with him, sharing a bottle of wine and a basket of bread before dinner.

Clearly, I may not be the only one in our relationship who is a poor judge of character.

"You two are still friends?"

Glen shows me his best forehand swing, the sleeve of his suit jacket riding up, exposing his wrist.

"Racquetball every other Thursday night at seven."

I turn back towards the window with the glass shelves. Down in front of the apartment complex where my car is parked I see something flipping up in the breeze, held down by the windshield wiper. Since finding the note under my doormat I'd dismissed it as a one-time prank. Quickly I scan the windshields of all the other cars parked at the curb, including Glen's gleaming black Tesla. Nothing is under the wipers.

CHAPTER SIX

I DRIVE TO A busy Whole Foods grocery store parking lot on Santa Monica Boulevard before unfolding the note. Part of me doesn't want to open it. Countless times I've read disturbing messages by a strange hand, but they've always been meant for someone other than me. I've been able to distance myself from the rage, the desperation, the incalculable danger in someone's words scribbled or written with too much care on the page. Killers, victims, false confessors, I'd profiled them all.

Whoever left this note under the wiper of my car had done so in broad daylight. *This person was following me.* For how long? Since I left the house this morning?

In under a couple seconds anyone could've come by and tucked the note under my wiper, someone posing as a jogger or a forgettable pedestrian taking a stroll down the sidewalk. During the day is when most of us let our guards down. Mid-afternoon, on a sunny Southern California day, Elise was physically taken from her driveway, cleanly, with nothing but her shoe left behind. More and more it looks like a kidnapping since it's been nearly two days without a word from her.

Presumably neither Glen or his assistant noticed the white paper under my car wiper when we'd gone our separate ways outside of the condominium complex. Glen's focus had been on me as he said his goodbyes, pushing for a kiss on my cheek while his assistant ignored me completely and made her way towards his Tesla, texting a message on her phone.

With shoppers teeming past the hood of my car, I am distracted by a young mother lifting her groceries into the trunk of her red Honda Civic while her toddler, a chubby boy in a baby blue jumper and denim newsboy cap, watches seated in the front of the shopping cart. He is content just wobbling back and forth, watching his mother as she loads bag after bag. The mother is wearing skintight yoga pants, a wind breaker and running shoes. After heading home she'll unpack the food and make her child a snack of sliced apples or a sandwich baggie of Cheerios before a leisurely stroller ride to the local park where this new mother will slowly rock back and forth on the swing, her little boy held close to her chest, essentially weightless in her arms, as if he's still a part of her body.

It isn't until she spots me staring at the two of them that I look back at the note in my lap, the one I still haven't read yet. That young mother couldn't possibly understand how lucky she is. If she did, she wouldn't turn her back on her little boy, not even for a second.

My hands are shaking and it's hard for me to focus. This second note changes things. It changes me. Instantly, whether I welcome it or not, I shed the years I've spent crunching and inflating numbers of properties all around L.A.

There is no possibility that I can dismiss this one as a prank. I will have to deliver the note to the police because it's no longer just about me. The words are all in caps this time, in black ballpoint instead of black felt tip.

ARE YOU HOPEFUL SHE IS STILL ALIVE?

At Copy Smart I slide my credit card into the plastic slot, pull up the cover of the machine and flatten the note face down on the glass, compromising the evidence. As soon as I read the indirect reference to Elise, I should've stopped handling the note on the off chance the writer had left his or her fingerprints.

The person behind the note strikes me as too clever for that. The neat block lettering reveals that much. He or she is precise. Deliberate. Educated. This is someone who makes very few mistakes.

I pull the first note from the side pocket of my purse where I've kept it since I found it on the front porch of my home.

He is here early.

Why change from the grammatically correct capital to lower case letters that comprised the sentence from the first note? Is it intentional to throw me off? Could there be two people behind the notes? Or is the writer more comfortable using all caps? Maybe he or she had written the second note in a rush. I pick up the original note from the copy machine and take a better look. The "H" in both notes share similarities, the same tight strokes, indicating it's possible they came from the same hand.

Besides making a copy of both notes, I'll also store a picture of them on my phone, though computers can't completely replicate a handwritten image, at least not to me. They will not hold the same potency on the screen as they do if I study them up close in hard copy.

I look up and take in who else is with me inside of the copy and postal service store. A guy in his twenties in baggy jeans and a black t-shirt is copying pages from a hefty hardback textbook. His back is to me. He looks like a college student, a book bag slung over one shoulder. Ear buds firmly in place, the cord dangles to the smart phone inside the back pocket of his pants. Further down, at the long panel of post office boxes, someone appears to be struggling to open up one of them with their key. From this distance, I can't tell if the person is a man or a woman.

Across from me, at the front counter, two female co-workers in cherry red Copy Smart polos are chatting up a storm, taking advantage of the slow afternoon in the store. Neither of them is particularly interested in me or what I'm doing either.

But I know the person who has brought me here is close by. The kind of people who write these notes aren't just toying with the recipient. They want attention. They want to brag. They want an intimacy on their terms with the person for whom the note is left. Above all, they want everyone to know for certain who is in control.

A boring dark blue sedan is parked next to Hugh's pick-up truck, which has two by four's neatly piled up in the flatbed, in the driveway of my home. Either Hugh is about to get caught red handed cheating on me with someone in law enforcement or Detective Ramirez is tired of the two of us playing phone tag.

He couldn't have chosen to come by at a worse time. I was planning on dropping both notes off tomorrow morning. How will he believe that now? No matter what I say it will appear like I'm withholding evidence. And Hugh will find out I never told him about the first note. He hates it when things are kept from him.

I park behind Hugh's truck because the detective has taken my spot.

Once inside the front door I hear the low masculine sounds of men talking, the words nearly inaudible unlike the women co-workers whose conversation I couldn't help but hear at Copy

Smart. The two men are in the family room, seated across from each other, the detective on the delicately embroidered Oriental couch my mother sent to me during her travels and Hugh in the ugly black leather recliner he brought from his apartment. Between my mother's well-meaning international gifts and Hugh gradually moving in, the décor of my home is positively schizophrenic, something the detective probably can't help but take note of. My fiancé is polite enough to make coffee for Detective Ramirez, but I see he passes on having a cup of his own.

Hugh stops paying attention to the detective when he sees me. His face is newly sunburned and his eyes show both confusion and concern. Already, before ever taking our vows, I've probably turned him around emotionally more times than his late wife during their over decade long marriage. Nobody takes a visit from the police lightly. I wonder if there are times, like right now, when Hugh finds himself second guessing why he's moved so fast on building a relationship with me, someone who keeps surprising him too often.

"Hey, Tia," he says. "This detective's here to ask you questions about that woman's disappearance."

The fact Hugh calls Elise "that woman" is another reminder how I've kept from him the part she is not just a client. She is a childhood friend.

Detective Ramirez rises from the couch. He's older like I figured with a thick head of graying hair combed back, a few extra pounds around his mid-section, and sharp dark eyes that make me think he's still a good shot.

In seconds, I feel him assess me as he shakes my hand, then lets it go, his mind already made up.

I notice a faded tattoo on the inside of his wrist, the writing indecipherable. He must've gotten inked in his youth, maybe gang related, maybe not, the meaning behind it no longer important. His cologne is familiar, an expensive brand I once bought Kyle for his birthday at Bloomingdale's in the Beverly Center. A woman loves him or used to. Detective Ramirez doesn't wear a ring, though most cops know better than to show any signs of their personal lives while on the job, considering the low life perps they deal with.

"I was on my way home to the Valley and I thought I'd drop by," he says as he takes his seat again. "Seems you and I are having some trouble speaking one-on-one."

That is enough to get Hugh to excuse himself and head into the other room. Another difference between Hugh and my ex-husband. Kyle would've insisted on sticking around for the police interview, not necessarily for support but because he doesn't ever like being the odd man out during a private conversation between two people.

I sit in Hugh's warm spot on the recliner and answer the obvious questions Detective Ramirez asks – about Elise's behavior while I estimated the worth of her father's estate. Did she receive any calls while I was with her? Did I notice any other cars parked outside that looked like they didn't belong? He writes my answers down on a pocket-size notepad.

"Have you talked to her father yet?" I can't help but ask.

Detective Ramirez doesn't look up from his notepad, busily jotting something down, though I am the one who asked a question. I imagine the words he writes oftentimes have extra gaps between them because he's constantly shifting from one train of thought to another.

"He's been kept up-to-date like the rest of the family."

"You've seen him *here* in LA?"

I think about telling Detective Ramirez the truth, that I witnessed, that *I heard* the awful sounds of Carson Davis hooked up to a life support machine, Elise's stoic, pregnant wife seated on guard at his bedside, but I realize I'd be wasting my time. The detective has already bought into the lie.

"He's on a boat, somewhere off the coast of Madrid, the Mediterranean. I don't know, something like that."

A boat?

The excuses the Davis Family or Elise's wife in particular have come up with sound incredible if it isn't for Carson's celebrity and wealth that make any outlandish location sound perfectly plausible.

"Her wife was there," I say. "With us at Carson's estate.

Have you asked her about that?"

The detective nods like I've offered nothing new.

"She mentioned she was with Elise that morning."

Finally, when it sounds like he's wrapping things up, I pull out the two notes, folded again, the way I'd found one of them.

"Someone left these for me," I begin. "One here under my welcome mat on the porch and the other earlier today while I was at an appraising job."

Detective Ramirez takes the notes and holds them close to his face with no concern that he might be blotting out possible trace evidence with his fat fingers.

He reads the first one out loud, then the second before turning them over like he expects to find something more.

"When did you say you got these?"

Was he hard of hearing?

"The first came a couple days ago. The other one was under the wiper of my car earlier this afternoon."

"Today?"

"Yes."

"You used to work for the police, downtown."

Either he has checked up on me before coming here or Hugh brought up to him what I used to do for a living. My fiancé might have figured that was why the detective had stopped by, to get me to analyze the hand of another criminal again. Before Detective Ramirez told Hugh about Elise being taken from her own driveway, that is.

"I was a handwriting profiler."

Shockingly Detective Ramirez tucks both

notes in the front pocket of his shirt, not slipping them into clear plastic evidence bags. Apparently, I had nothing to worry about earlier in the copy center when I made duplicates of the notes.

"You used to read into this kind of sh…stuff years ago?"

The way he poses the question, stopping himself before he says the word *shit* shouldn't get to me. Most men casually curse no matter how serious the issue. But I can sense, to him, handwriting analysis is right up there with online psychics and telepathy experts with hotline numbers that charge by the minute.

And in some way, he's right. It is as imprecise as it can be accurate. He must pride himself as the kind of seasoned cop that arrests suspects with logical, less speculative evidence – fingerprints and faulty alibis.

What good would it do if I told him about how I'd helped police recover a murder weapon through the written statement of a thirty-two-year old man suspected of shooting his mother once in the temple in a badly staged suicide. Nothing valuable had actually been taken, not even the one karat diamond wedding ring off the dead woman's finger.

After studying the son's statement where he denied emphatically that he'd been anywhere near the home they shared when the crime occurred, I noticed at the end of his words that ended with 'r' that the letter was detached from the rest each time. A sign, some might interpret, of an unconscious confession, the 'r' referring to something he couldn't shake from his psyche. I determined it might be the location where he'd disposed of the murder weapon. Three days later the gun was recovered by police in the shallow waters of the concrete channel of the Los Angeles River, a few miles from the residence.

There is a brief silence between the detective and me, the two of us sizing one another up. But then Hugh startles us both by barging into the room. He's listened to some if not all of our conversation and he's not happy about it. His dark expression is foreign even to me and he's pointing at the detective the way an enraged driver does right after he pops out of the car and a physical fight is about to break out. Gone is the civility of poured coffee and casual talk.

"The person who left these fucked up notes for my fiancée could be responsible for taking that woman?"

Detective Ramirez is on his feet, on instinct, at the sound of another man's anger.

"Could be. The story's been on the news a couple days now."

He shrugs, then momentarily glances at me before focusing back on Hugh. The detective moves towards the front door. He knows he's worn out his welcome. He opens the front door, looks out at his unmarked sedan parked in the gravel driveway, then he turns to Hugh and me as if he's forgotten to mention one last detail in Elise's case.

"Might be someone looking for a little attention. I wouldn't worry too much yet. Be cautious.

Lock the doors. Call me if you get another one."

I see it in his stare before he turns his back and walks away from us. *Might be someone looking for a little attention.*

What I am expecting is to get read the riot act for not coming forth sooner with the notes. It hasn't occurred to me Detective Ramirez might think I am pathetic enough to falsify them in order to inject myself all these years later into another high-profile case.

CHAPTER SEVEN

HUGH WAITS UNTIL I'm buckled into the passenger seat of his pick-up and we're headed to El Coyote for dinner before he brings it up. Shortly after Detective Ramirez left Hugh suggested we go out to eat at one of our favorite Mexican restaurants as if this was like any other evening and he hadn't just lost his temper and cursed at a cop. Hugh knows every side street to take in order to avoid the worst of the evening traffic. Narrowly we accelerate past homes cramped next to one another with lights filling the front windows and cars lined up on either side of the curbs. More than once the tires of his truck have screeched during a turn before he remembers to let up on the gas.

I put my hand against the dash for balance.

He is upset with me.

"At what point, Tia, were you going to tell me you're being stalked?"

"I'm not sure whether it's *stalking*," I say. "Someone just left me a couple of notes.

"What would you call it then?"

I don't answer him because I don't know whether the notes are just a sick prank or if there's someone out there I really need to be scared of. Could it be the same person who took Elise from her driveway?

ARE YOU HOPEFUL SHE IS STILL ALIVE?

If it is the same person, there is the chilling possibility that he or she might be confessing in that one line that they've already killed her. That would be one way, the worst way, to decipher the message in the note.

Out the passenger window I see two young girls riding bicycles one behind the other on the sidewalk, at dusk, when they should've been called in by their parents for dinner by now. So many families mistakenly think they're safe in their own neighborhoods, that they have locks on their doors and the police are just a 911 call away.

But I learned years before that danger is not only down the block.

It can actually find a way inside your house. You may even unknowingly welcome that danger right inside your own front door.

"Detective Ramirez doesn't sound too concerned about it," I finally say to Hugh. "We probably shouldn't either."

His hands grip the wheel even tighter. A scab has built up on his right knuckle, one that hadn't been there when he and I were in bed the other night. He is the kind of contractor that would rather work up on the roof with his employees than bark orders at them from the ground.

"You should've told me."

"You're right," I say, hoping he'll leave it alone

if I agree with him. "I should've told you."

Hugh turns on to Beverly Boulevard, then suddenly brakes hard to avoid hitting the rear bumper of a Mercedes that cuts into our lane. El Coyote is only a couple blocks away, though I'm not sure if we'll make it there without both of us getting banged up.

"I don't care about being right, Tia. I just don't want to see you get hurt. You should move into my apartment."

Even though I knew one was coming, this isn't the argument I'd imagined. There's no way I'm letting anyone, whether it's a freak sending me notes or my very own fiancé, scare me out of my own home.

"If this person is really stalking me, as you say, what makes you think I'll be safe at your place when you have to go off to work?"

Hugh looks annoyed at me for being logical, for once.

"I don't know why you keep saying *this person*."

"And you know who it is?"

Hugh shakes his head as if he can't believe why I haven't figured it out too.

"Your husband called earlier while you were out. I answered the phone."

"Ex, Hugh. Knock it off."

"No," he corrects me. "I mean your husband. That's what he called himself. He said the two of you met the other day for lunch."

For some reason it feels like I'm caught in a lie, and I don't like it. Hugh has no right to dictate where I go or who I see. Besides there is nothing left between Kyle and me but a shared asset in our divorce decree.

"It was over property. Nothing else."

"Right."

"Why would Kyle send me creepy notes?"

"You don't get it."

Hugh drives right past the valet who is expecting us to park the car with him and finds his own spot in the back of the lot next to a shiny Porsche. He kills the engine, then looks at me with such determination that whatever he says next will be the end of this line of conversation.

"That son of a bitch ex-husband of yours *wants* you to feel like you're not safe with me."

Over a dinner of soft tacos and salty margaritas, virgin for me, just in case I'm pregnant, Hugh and I try and find our way back to the moment before Detective Ramirez showed up hours earlier to my home. Before Elise's suede pump was dropped in her driveway and every local news channel is now covering the search in the Hollywood Hills for her body. Before the two handwritten notes left to rattle me, to show that the sick individual behind them could track me wherever I go, *that I'm easily found*.

Three days earlier things had been normal, at least, normal for us. We were doing our best to blend our lives together, to start planning our wedding and move forward.

The restaurant is packed, the walls festively decorated with sombreros, framed drawings of women dressed in flowery Spanish dresses, the rise and fall of men shouting from the bar where they're watching a Lakers game. With all the noise it's easy to allow for a lull in the conversation between Hugh and me. Our waitress passes by the table with a sizzling plate of fajitas for the booth behind us. On her way back to the kitchen Hugh stops her and asks for a straight shot of vodka.

He looks troubled like his mind has snagged on something he can't let go of.

I'm not up for another argument about Kyle.

"I appraised a set of duplexes for Glen not far from here," I say. I've done what I do well, I've changed the subject. I fill the air with conversation to avoid talking about anything than what is behind Hugh's stoic expression.

He glances at me like the name doesn't register.

"Glen said you two play racquetball every other Thursday."

Hugh just nods. All I get is a nod before he looks away, probably in search of our waitress and his order.

"I didn't know you were friends with him." I can't help but keep pushing. "I didn't even know you knew him, actually."

The waitress returns with the shot and Hugh downs it in one forced swallow.

I'm not used to seeing him this tense, drinking hard liquor, especially on a week night. Being hung over on a fifteen-foot ladder puts even the most skillful construction worker in a precarious position and Hugh is not the type to just stand around on a site. Finally, he stops avoiding eye contact like he's ready to be straight with me.

"Glen's more of a business acquaintance, Tia. I let him win most of our games and he mentions me to his high rent clients who are looking to renovate inside and out or bulldoze the multimillion-dollar properties they just bought."

I smile.

"You let him win?"

Hugh chuckles. His cheeks are flushed from the sudden rush of alcohol in his system.

"You've seen the guy's ego. Of course, I let him win. It's not easy either because he's one slow son of a bitch on the court. Major marathon runner, my ass."

I laugh too. Making a joke at Glen's expense further distances my fiancé from him. The date nights with their spouses seem more long ago than when Glen spoke earlier about them.

Hugh turns the empty shot glass in his hand.

"I'm sorry," he says. "I didn't mean to jump all over you about Kyle. That cop showing up at the house today…"

Hugh shakes his head like he's picturing images he doesn't want to see. Several squad cars in front of the home he once shared with his family, his little girl crying, later his wife's body being pulled out of a drawer at the morgue for him to officially identify as the next of kin.

"I just can't be sure…"

I touch his wrist.

The thick cords of his veins leading up his arm resemble the outward strength of a body builder's from over thirty years spent pounding nails under the blazing sun. Inside, though, he's a wounded man, a loving husband who, without warning, lost his wife one afternoon. Even now the hurt in his eyes shows he may never fully heal.

"It's okay, Hugh."

I understand the reason for his ordering a shot of vodka.

His late wife was home alone when she'd accidentally drowned in their backyard pool they'd recently just had put in. She'd misjudged how shallow it was when she dove off the edge and cracked her head on the bottom, losing consciousness. Their daughter was in school. Hugh had been on an ocean front site, a couple hours away in Santa Barbara when it happened, when his wife's lungs lethally filled with chlorine water.

He didn't share any of that with me until four weeks into dating. Guilt is a chronic emotion that lingers in the body like a disease in remission, just waiting to resurface.

I know what my fiancé must be thinking.

If he couldn't protect his own wife from accidentally drowning, how can he protect me from the disturbed person who is taunting me with those notes?

CHAPTER EIGHT

~Back Then~

FIVE DAYS AFTER his sexual encounter with my friend, Jordan caught up with me as I was leaving my Gender Studies class. It was a dull lecture hall class that most students showed up for but instead of taking notes students usually checked email or listened to music on their ear buds. The female professor didn't care, speaking mostly to the screen where her notes were projected instead of towards her actual audience. It was as if she, too, had given up on teaching the subject to her students.

"Hey," he said, swerving in front of me on his skateboard. In one fluid move, he pressed down on the tail of his board and caught it in one hand. "Catia, right?"

I nodded. I wasn't sure what he wanted from me, maybe for me to give a message to Jessica for him since her jock boyfriend was back in town. The well-worn skateboard and frayed cargo shorts didn't throw me off. Jordan's parents were loaded and probably spoiled him in every way possible. One night at a party he bragged that his haircut cost a hundred and fifty bucks, some salon in Costa Mesa his mother drove him to every six weeks.

Jordan let out a loud construction worker's whistle

like a pretty girl had just passed by.

"Professor Larkin is one angry lesbo. I had to take that class freshman year. Twice. My parents wouldn't let me get away with the C she gave me." He made a high-pitched woman's voice and wagged his finger. "I could care less whether she's a dyke and dislikes you because you have a scrotum, young man. You must be above women like her. You have law school to think of."

I wondered if he was quoting his mother word for word and she threw around such offensive language so easily about people she didn't know.

"Professor Larkin is married," I said quietly in case she came out of the hall and overheard us, "to a man." I was earning an A- in the class and I'd been to her office where she had a wedding photo of her and her husband on the desk, oddly facing out towards whoever sat down across from her. Now I understood why. Just because she taught Gender Studies, she was oftentimes stereotyped as being gay.

Jordan cocked his head to the side, frustrated, it seemed, that I corrected him about Professor Larkin or that his little story about her didn't charm me.

"You don't like me much, do you."

I started walking like I was in a hurry even though I had two hours between classes.

"It's not that," I said, stupidly suggesting that there was something that made me not like him. I was not so naïve not to realize that my innocence was a challenge to him, and yet I found his interest in me flattering.

"Let me take you to lunch," he said, now balancing on his board in order to keep up with me. "I bet I can change your mind about me before you're done eating."

We went to a restaurant with tables out in front, off

campus, ordered double decker hamburgers and split a basket of fries. We talked for hours and I missed my next class, World Literature, without realizing it. He told me more about his "tight-assed" parents and I let him know about my father dying when I was twelve, a freak brain aneurism when he was an otherwise healthy thirty-seven-year old man.

My mother had kissed my father goodnight, rolled over, and in the morning when she tried to wake him, he was cold to the touch. 911 was called and soon my sister and I were awakened to the sound of first responders. My mother must've heard me ask what was wrong from the other side of the shared wall, because she ordered me, in the form of a primal scream deep inside her chest, not to come out of my bedroom.

Laney crept from her room, into my bed and together, under the covers, we listened, not sure what was happening but knowing it was something that was going to change our lives forever. Then our mother suddenly appeared in the doorway, temporarily composed, and told us to get dressed. She went to my closet and ripped clothes off their hangers, two different blouses, a nice dress I wore to church for Greek Easter, items that did not go together yet she laid them on my unmade bed before she just stopped.

It was as if she'd had a change of heart, and she broke down, sobbing, on her knees, beside the bed, saying she couldn't handle seeing him leave our home that way, not all alone.

She needed her two kores with her.

I remembered thinking she wasn't making any sense. Her large black eyes that everyone complimented her on darted from me to Laney as if she couldn't concentrate on either one of us. It was a lack of focus from which she'd never fully recover. I could smell her bad morning breath that came out in hollow bursts. Then she held each of our hands and took us to her bedroom and we saw his body covered in a white sheet, being carried out on a gurney with a squeaky wheel.

This became the surest memory I carried with me about my father's abrupt death — my mother's unpredictable heartbreak. Later after selling off my father's business, she'd attend church, Bible study, and socialize at practically all of their potlucks, doing everything she could to pray her way of out her near crippling grief.

Year after year, Laney and I became more doubtful any of it was actually helping.

I left that part out to Jordan.

I left out another part too, how I chased after the paramedics, how one of them had to grab my arms to keep me from yanking off the sheet. My father wouldn't die on me, not just after I'd graduated into the seventh grade. We planned a camping trip to Yosemite with tents, nightly campfires, roasted hot dogs and gooey marshmallows two and a half weeks from then. I'd been counting down on my Snoopy wall calendar. Other friends' fathers were waking up and going to work like it was any other day, fathers who were not in nearly as good of physical shape as mine.

"Man, you never hear about people who aren't, you know, grandpa old, actually dying in their sleep," Jordan piped in, having only been told the surface level facts of my father's death. "That's fucking crazy."

That weekend Jordan took me to a movie, skipping out on the party his frat house was throwing. Jessica and her boyfriend would be there, along with my other *friends. But I kept it secret why I couldn't go with them. I lied to my mother too when she called earlier that day. I told her I'd be in the library that smelled of moldy old books, studying for a test.*

In the theater with the lights dimming, Jordan hooked his arm around my neck and slowly pulled me close. I smelled his near sickening breath from the runny cheese and jalapeno nachos he'd been snacking on.

"Kiss me with your eyes open," he'd whispered to me. "I don't want you thinking about me in bed with your friend."

CHAPTER NINE

NOT ONLY DOES Hugh stay the night, he's still here at the house when I wake up at seven. I hear him moving around on the hard-wood floor downstairs. The startling sounds of another person living with me is something I'll have to get used to again. After Kyle left the quiet seemed deafening. My fiancé's crew has been at the Malibu site without him for at least an hour which must be killing him thinking of the mistakes being made that he could easily correct if he was there to witness them.

From the bedroom window, when I part the curtains, I have full view of the gravel drive and both our vehicles parked out front. No note on my windshield or on Hugh's truck for that matter, just a sheen of morning dew on the glass, the first sign of fall in Southern California, though the beam of morning light in my face makes it feel like it might turn out to be another warm day.

Should a new note appear the pattern will most likely remain the same, meaning it will be found in a different, possibly closer spot which worries me. So far whoever it is has kept some distance, the outside of my car, the front porch of my home. Next time would this person go so far as to break in to my house?

I let go of the curtain, then change into a pair of destructed jean shorts and a black sleeveless blouse before heading downstairs.

The local news is playing on TV in the family room when I enter with a cup of coffee. Hugh is sitting forward in that awful black recliner. He's dressed for the Malibu site, down to his well-worn jeans and work boots that are speckled with dried cement. Apparently, he's been waiting for me to wake up before he leaves.

"What is it?" I say.

"They found a bone yesterday in the hills where they searched for that woman you know."

"A bone?"

I sit on the arm of the recliner and Hugh rubs the small of my back. His touch is soothing, the touch of a man who cared for his little girl when she was sick with a high fever or held her hand with rock solid protectiveness graveside as her mother was put to rest. The touch of a hands-on father. No matter what my fiancé is convinced that Kyle is up to, I do feel safe with Hugh. He is a man who is unafraid of standing up to a detective, intimidating him into making a hasty retreat out of our home.

"Could be human or animal," he says. "They aren't sure yet."

This is actually good news. In a particularly startling case I'd helped the police with, the woman had been decapitated, the rest of her body left along a shallow edge of the Angeles Forest. Her fingers were taken too to avoid easy identification or maybe to make a statement that the woman's talent as an artist was gone now along with her life. No more high strokes or careful blotting with the brush that somehow resembled shapes and figures. She painted as did her husband, the kind of art work that sold for six figures at auctions and in chic galleries where the public wasn't invited. An appointment must be made first just to view it. Her older husband had killed her. He didn't have another woman on the side. No, he was afraid his younger wife was about to surpass his longstanding success and he couldn't have that. His career was on the decline while hers was on the rise. His alibi had been that he was on a business trip to secure a showing of his work in a gallery in San Diego, a couple hours' drive from their home on the canal in Venice. Investigators gave me a copy of the hotel bill he'd signed, an erratic scribble compared to the rest of the samples of his handwriting they'd given me to assess. The extra darkness of his name alone when I traced over it with my fingertip may as well have been his confession. I felt how hard down he'd pressed. I felt his pent-up rage, his self-hatred and capability for violence. With my findings as well as the relatively good condition of the rest of her remains, minus the parts he'd removed and were never recovered, it was determined she'd died within the time frame of him murdering her right before he went on his trip. The police were also able to get out of the husband his intense jealousy that made him so sick inside that he murdered a woman he claimed to still love. Turned out it was late when he'd deposited her body. Jumbled up in the head, exhausted and anxious someone might see him, he assumed he'd left her further enough in the woods so she wouldn't immediately be found. He was wrong.

"It isn't her," I say to Hugh. "Elise hasn't been gone long enough for her body to decompose that quickly. Even if the wildlife got to it."

On screen a petite woman in her thirties, with a black pixie cut and a good lip injection job, is speaking but her voice is muted. The reporter's voice can be heard instead going on about a number people may call if they have seen Elise's dark gray SUV. The woman with the pixie cut is standing in front of what looks like a clothing store, and I suddenly have a good idea of who she is.

It's taken the media over three days to track her down. How long will it take for them to find out their divorce is nearly finalized or have they found out already? Is that why a reporter is talking over the footage of her? Soon-to-be-exes may hold some value being seen though not necessarily heard.

A spokesman for the police department is now on the air saying the similar thing I just said to Hugh, that they were following up on a tip, but instead have possibly found traces of another unsolved crime. Basically, the police have no idea where Elise could be. If it isn't a kidnapping for ransom, then someone who wants to hurt the

Davis Family is behind Elise's disappearance.

Quite possibly the kidnapper doesn't know about Carson's medical condition, one of the best kept celebrity secrets since Rock Hudson withheld from the public his homosexuality and later his HIV diagnosis, the news finally breaking at the worst time, in the '80s, when hysteria over the disease was at an all-time high. Shortly after my father died, my mother and I watched old films late at night when she couldn't sleep. I wanted to keep her company. Our favorites of Rock Hudson's were the drama *Magnificent Obsession* with Jane Wyman and the epic Western *Giant* co-starring Elizabeth Taylor.

It might not be a kidnapper at all. Perhaps it's a cold- blooded killer who is sticking around, toying with me because he knows he can, because he knows about my background and that I might be able to trace his words back to him and he'll be caught. The BTK Killer who bound, tortured and killed his victims in the Midwest lay dormant for several years before suddenly sending detailed information about his killings to a TV station only to have those messages tracked by the police to the church where he served as an elder. It's not so much getting caught that concerns such a killer. It's the public confession that they long for, the recounting of their grisly crimes they get to replay over and over again behind bars.

Before Hugh leaves I make him a quick breakfast of scrambled eggs and toast while he heads outside to check things out one last time before being gone for the rest of the day. While

I'm cooking, I multi-task, turning on my smart phone and typing in the name of Carson's third wife inside the box of the search engine.

An article pops up, nearly two years before.

Mrs. Carson Davis, Gia Nivens-Davis 31, opens Distraction Boutique on Melrose Avenue.

I click on the link and there is a picture of Gia posing with Carson during the ribbon cutting. He's tall and fatherly, standing beside his beaming bride – no physical signs of the illness to come that would abruptly change everything, leaving him bedridden and on a ventilator. They each hold a pair of scissors nearly the size of gardening shears.

Clearly, he was an active part of her life then. Elise's wife Deborah had made it sound like they'd been separated for much longer. She'd called Gia, "A greedy young flight attendant he'd brought home from a trip to Kauai." By Deborah's dismissive estimation, carting back a box of pineapples would've proven more useful.

I recognize the same storefront of the footage from her on the local news today. The boutique offers off the rack styles from top of the line designers and promises dresses can be ordered for formal occasions as well.

I hear the front door open, then quickly close.

"Nothing?" I call out to Hugh.

"All clear."

Hugh comes into the kitchen, eyeing my legs and the frayed threads dangling from the hem of my jean shorts.

"What are you up to today?" He wraps his

arms around me, then digs his hands down into my back pockets, pulling me in close. "I take it you're not showing up for an appraisal job wearing these."

I can't tell if I hear disapproval in his voice or if he's just teasing me about dressing so casually. There is a generational gap between us, the difference between what his late wife probably wore – thigh covering walking shorts, and what I have on, skin flashing cutoffs. At the moment I'm dressed more like his eighteen-year-old daughter living in a dorm at Washington State. My younger age makes it an unspoken rule that I must tread lightly on the periphery of her life as "her friend" and never act like a real stepparent. It's why a part of me is grateful she isn't coming home for a visit until Thanksgiving.

"Taking the day off to shop for a wedding dress."

"You'll be gorgeous in anything."

I look away, still unable to take one of his sincere compliments head on.

"I wouldn't go that far."

"I would."

To Hugh it must sound like I'm thinking only about our future. But it's also partly about my past, my childhood I spent with Elise, how if she were truly dead I'd be the only one left to live with the unthinkable truth she and I shared.

Jessica goes with me to Distraction Boutique. We've remained friends through college, her many breakups with guys, who, like her, call off the relationship before it gets too serious. When I phoned her in tears telling her I was divorcing Kyle she bluntly and unapologetically said, "Good, I never liked that arrogant dick." But she's also been pretty damn loyal to me. For several nights in a row she stayed on the line with me, sometimes until dawn, talking me through the initial raw emotions of my failed marriage.

When I fell headfirst in love with Hugh mere weeks after Kyle and I separated, she kept the obvious possibility I was rushing into another relationship to herself. After our engagement two months after we'd first met, she'd bit her sharp tongue, simply suggesting a longer engagement might be easier on Hugh's daughter. In quick translation it also meant she wanted to make sure I knew what I was getting into with an older man, a widower with a teenage daughter who'd lost her mother not that long ago. Resentment at her father moving on with another woman might strike out of the blue and I would catch the brunt of it. Why would I intentionally put myself through all that?

Emotional baggage of any kind, including her own, makes Jessica nervous. Now she has a successful long-distance entanglement with a guy in the Bay area. Every other weekend she flies north for great sex and Sunday brunch. She runs her own interior design business in Westwood, catering to mostly law firms and corporate businesses downtown. Her clients pay her plenty, so she can get away whenever she pleases such as coming with me on a second's notice to do a little shopping.

The boutique is between a coffee house with a canopy, and wooden tables and chairs on the sidewalk and an alley lined with dumpsters belonging to the businesses in front.

Jessica looks up at the sign of the third Mrs. Carson Davis's boutique. Her hair is pulled back in a rubber band and she's wearing yoga pants and a long t-shirt to cover up the added pounds to her midsection from her self-indulgent roundtrips to San Francisco.

"Please tell me again why we're going into a clothing store that sounds more like a nightclub?"

I laugh and point a finger at her.

"Don't embarrass me."

Jessica feigns innocence.

"What'd I say, Tia?"

I open the front door and instantly notice the sparse luxury of a high-end retail store. In the center of the room is a tan leather couch and two glass end tables. On a longer table against the wall is a stainless-steel espresso machine with a stack of ceramic white cups and saucers. The racks along the walls are lined with dresses and skirts perfectly spaced out on puffy hangers. One black skirt with chiffon ruffles along the bottom is red marked on sale for a cool three hundred dollars.

The third Mrs. Carson Davis has good taste.

A young woman with shoulder length blonde hair parted down the middle greets us wearing a bright blue V-neck blouse and matching skirt. She's in uncomfortably high black patent leather heels and her face is made up like a runway model – perfect foundation and blush, heavily made up smoky eyes and red lipstick, absolutely untouchable. She probably doesn't drink or eat all day until her shift is over.

"May I help you two ladies?" she asks politely, knowing better than to size up our buying possibilities by our casual clothes.

I lay out to her that I'm interested in a basic but tasteful cocktail dress appropriate for a second wedding. Within minutes I am in a spacious dressing stall with four different dresses, all in my size, size 2, without me having to tell the saleswoman.

For the next half hour, I try on dress after dress from a white strapless lace dress, a conservative velvet number that makes me look more like the mother of the bride than the bride herself, to the ivory slip dress I've just fit over my head and shimmied down my body. The bottom hem of the dress lands at my ankles. The fabric is so smooth I see my hip bones and small breasts, my two biggest flaws. I hate it, but I step out of the stall anyway so Jessica may have a look.

"That's gorgeous," she says, sipping from the complimentary espresso the saleswoman whipped up for her. "Your body makes me sick. You're as skinny as a model and I doubt you're starving yourself like one."

We're both staring at each other in the full-length three-way mirror outside of the dressing rooms.

I grin and put a hand on my stomach that is so flat it pretty much sinks in.

"Two tacos and a ton of salsa and chips last night, plus a virgin margarita."

"Virgin? So you're—?"

I shake my head. The knowledge I'm still not pregnant stuns me the way it always does. I think of Elise's wife Deborah and her full womb. I think of the abortion Jessica had when we were seniors in college, the fetus she so coldly paid to have cleansed from her uterus because it got in the way of her future plans. I think of my three healthy young nephews. Laney has never had any trouble getting pregnant. In fact, her husband is thinking about getting a vasectomy in order to stop their family from growing any more.

"But I might be by the time we marry," I add to Jessica, filling the silence between us with false promise. Four failed pregnancy tests I've discarded in the garbage since being intimate with Hugh, yet he reassures me we're just getting started. "Maybe I should hold off on the dress."

Jessica's expression turns like she wants to say something but thinks better of it.

"Nope. This is the one. You can always order an extra in a larger size. I bet you'll be one of those obnoxious women who doesn't even look pregnant from behind."

Her quick explanation doesn't matter so much as what I hear in her voice, the doubt, the practical certainty that there is no chance I'll be pregnant with Hugh's baby by next summer.

At the front counter as I'm paying for the dress, the woman I came here to see suddenly appears from the back where there must be an office. The current Mrs. Carson Davis, Gia Nivens-Davis. She's as carefully put together as her employee, wearing a black pencil skirt that makes her petite frame even shorter and an ivory blouse with a neckline so plunging I wonder if she's had to use tape to hold the blouse down from flashing the public. Oddly enough, on her ring finger is a hefty diamond. If she is nearly divorced, why is she still wearing her wedding ring?

Gia glances at the ivory slip dress the saleswoman is placing in the garment bag, then she assesses me.

"That dress will look beautiful on you. You definitely have the figure for it."

"Thanks," I say.

The saleswoman hands back my credit card.

In the next few seconds I'll need to somehow bring up Gia's connection with Elise or else I'll lose my chance. Stupidly I realize I should have gone over beforehand what I'd say to her if I actually saw her.

"I'm sorry," I say so softly I'm not sure she's heard me.

Gia concentrates on me a little harder now. No longer am I just a customer, I'm someone who's *recognized* her, a former flight attendant who used to fly out of Kauai.

Money is not the only reason why some women are drawn to well-known men.

"What?"

I clear my throat. I need to say something about her connection to Elise and I need to say it right now.

"I saw you on the news this morning. That was you, wasn't it?"

Jessica, who stands next to me, looks up from thumbing a message on her smart phone, her attention officially grabbed. Maybe she's aware of Elise's story. For the past couple days, it's dominated the news cycle. Even the nationwide morning news shows have picked up the story. I've never told Jessica about my friendship with Elise. There's never been any reason to since I've been friends with them at different times of my life.

"My stepdaughter," is all Gia says as if I should be able to fill in the rest.

"Must be around your age," Jessica butts in, finishing her sentence for her. "You two are probably close? More like friends?"

Leave it to Jessica to ask a nosy question and save the day.

"Very close," Gia stresses without backing it up with any personal anecdote. "It's a terrible time for us. But the police are doing a thorough job and we have every reason to believe she'll be returned safely."

Us?

"You and Carson?" I blurt out.

Gia looks at me like she can't believe my question. Her shock is hard to read. It could be real or it could be for show. In the last couple of days, with at least one media interview, she's had time to practice.

"Of course, my husband and me."

She says this like Carson is waiting for her at home, on the couch with his feet up, a tumbler of whiskey in hand, when in fact, I know he's somewhere flat on his back in a hospital bed, unconscious and hooked to life support.

I take the receipt, then the garment bag from the saleswoman. With my transaction complete I face the not-so-subtle saleswoman wishing me a good rest of my day.

But I can't let it go, not when I've caught Gia in a lie.

"I thought I read somewhere that the two of you were separated."

She puts her hand with the big rock on it to her bare chest. The most dramatic yet predictable women always seem to have their fake nails painted the color of fresh blood. Kyle's freak new girlfriend's nails were done a dingy white, the decision behind it as strange and unexplainable as her.

"Absolutely not." Gia acts horrified at the presumption. "I don't know which *rag* you read that in. He's been out of the country, isolated, hard at work on a memoir about his life. He's devastated about what's happened to his daughter."

I force out an apology because it seems, given the circumstances, that I must. But what she says compounds the lie told last night on the news, the public statement supposedly made by Carson. It is as fake as her blood red nails, as her sham of a marriage, as her put on sorrow at her stepmother's disappearance. The man cannot write one word because he is lying unconscious in a hospital bed, unable to even breathe on his own. If I voice what I know, I will look like the crazy person even to Jessica. As I walk out of the boutique, I realize there isn't a single member of the Davis Family that has told me the truth.

CHAPTER TEN

KYLE IS SEATED on the porch steps of my home as I drive up after having dropped off Jessica back at her place in West L.A. He's in jeans and a black t-shirt, the markedly casual, go-to way he'd dress whenever we'd hit the farmer's market on the weekend or a light breakfast of egg white omelets at Mel's on Sunset. Only it's not a Saturday or Sunday morning. It's a weekday afternoon and Kyle and I aren't together any-more. We're legally divorced. Hanging on a hook in the backseat is my new wedding dress, the fit so perfect Jessica went on and on during the car ride home that it doesn't even need to be altered.

I shut off the engine and for a moment I sit in the car, absorbing the fact my ex-husband has shown up unexpectedly at my door. What is he doing here? Giving in about fixing up the Marina Del Rey condo before selling it was a mistake. The deed with both our names on it still keeps a connection between us, one the divorce was supposed to sever. But I've never been very con-sistent at holding my ground and Kyle knows it.

When I get out with the garment bag from Distraction Boutique, I scan the front passenger seat of his Mercedes, surprised to see he's made the trip alone, without Becca. She doesn't strike me as the type who lets him out of her sight for very long. He must not have told her he was coming by.

Kyle notices the heavy plastic in my arms with a see-through patch of ivory satin showing, yet he says nothing.

Instead he waves awkwardly like a stranger, like a man who hasn't bravely swam naked with me in the cold white caps of the Atlantic in the middle of the night because we were tired of watching the water from five stories above on our hotel balcony. Not like the man who pushed me up against a wall in the home right behind where he stands now and we had sex mere feet from the bedroom and our bed because, for some reason, we just had to.

"I would've called." He shrugs, getting up off the steps. "But I already tried that a couple of times."

Do I talk with him outside or do I let him in? If any of the neighbors, as far away as they are, glimpse the two of us out here they may leap to the idea we've gotten back together.

If they happen to hear either of us raise our voices, they'll really think we're an item again. But it wasn't always like that. Together we changed what had once been a beat-up two-bedroom rental with a rickety front porch into a quaint, cozy vintage home worthy of a Laurel Canyon address. We spent weekends and called in sick days at work in order to retile the bathroom, rebuild the front deck with sturdy cedar planks, rip up the carpets and stain the hardwood floors until they shone brand new. We worked the same crazy hours, sometimes most of the night, until lifting a paint brush felt too heavy or we were too bleary-eyed to hammer a nail straight. At one time Kyle and I shared the same goals. We'd been an unmatchable team.

"I've had my phone off today," I say, brushing past him towards the front door. "I was running errands with Jessica." He still smells of the cologne I bought him for his birthday that year from Bloomingdales, the cologne I recognized on Detective Ramirez the other day. The cologne Kyle will continue wearing while he's naked in bed with Becca or any other woman because it's his scent now and it has nothing to do with me.

"How's she doing?" He laughs. "Or rather who is she doing?"

My back is to my ex so he doesn't see me smile.

"A financial advisor in San Francisco."

Kyle comes closer, touching the garment bag draped over my arm.

"Can I take that?"

"I can manage," I say, entering the house and laying the garment bag on Hugh's black recliner. I turn, catching my ex eyeing some of the minor changes to the house since his departure, the bulky recliner, the new rug in the foyer my mother sent me from Southeast Asia, Cambodia, I think it was.

"Nice chair," he comments, patting the back of it. "Definitely dresses up the place."

"Why are you here?" I ask.

Kyle digs both hands in the front pockets of his jeans.

He's still looking at the chair, Hugh's chair.

"I need you to appraise a client's three bedroom for me in Encino." He turns his attention back on to me. "Jesus, Tia. You're sounding a little paranoid. Everything okay?"

No, things are not okay, but I'll be damned if I tell my ex-husband that. My childhood friend is missing and someone is leaving me cryptic notes, possibly related to the crime. It is just like Kyle and his professorial ego to think I won't mind if he stops by, that being my ex-husband gives him some sort of privileges. That only works if you share a child and Kyle wouldn't give me one of those.

"Hugh told me you called yesterday. You really need to stop screwing with him."

"Seriously? That's what he told you?"

Kyle runs a hand through his bangs, then shuts the front door like he's not going anywhere until he says what he's come here to say.

"I asked to speak with you, that's all. So, what? Now I can't offer you any work because he's in the picture? Is that it? That guy's more insecure than I thought."

I head deeper down the foyer into the kitchen where I'll pull out some pots and pans to give the impression I'm about to start dinner and Kyle should leave soon. He doesn't get the hint. He grabs a glass from the cabinet and fills it halfway with water from the dispenser on the fridge door, the way he always used to. Then he sits on one of three stools that line the counter top. The familiarity of my ex-husband in *my home* is jarring because he no longer belongs here, and I suddenly forget why I'd opened the cabinet stacked with plates, saucers and cups.

I turn, desperately wishing he'd just leave now.

"There's a vigil tomorrow night for Elise Davis," Kyle says. He drinks from the glass of water. "You two went to middle school together or something, right?"

"Yes, how'd you–"

"I know you like to think I never listened to you, but on occasion I actually did." He takes another swallow, then sets the glass back down on the counter where he'll leave it for me to clear. "Maybe I'll see you there."

"You're going?" I stare at my ex-husband, really look at him. He appears jittery, worn out, buzzed from lack of sleep. Something or *someone* is stressing him out, though if it's Becca that's a problem he willingly asked for.

"Why not?" Kyle says. "It's at Carson Davis's estate. They're going to open the doors to the grounds. Obviously, the house will be off limits. Rumor is his place is about to go up for sale. Fuck, what I wouldn't do to snag that listing, especially now."

I let that last comment at Elise's expense go. It isn't Kyle's business to know I was the one who'd appraised the home. He might already suspect it.

"I keep hearing stories about your friend, Elise. She has more dirt in her own backyard than a

Malibu resident after a mudslide." Kyle callously laughs at his own bad joke. "Man, she's crossed a lot of people."

"Please, just stop."

Kyle sees I'm not up to trash talk my missing friend. I honestly don't know enough about her life now to either agree or disagree with him.

"So we're good with the Encino three bedroom?"

I nod.

"I'll text you with the details. If you could do it by late next week that'd be great."

"Nothing like giving me some time, Kyle."

He hops off the stool, then puts a hand to his chest like I've hurt his feelings somehow.

"Hey, I do my best. You know how rabid these types can be when they get it in their minds they want to sell."

Rarely does Kyle put down his clients. Usually he's too busy envying their assets. As he lets himself out and I hear the front door close, I suddenly question Kyle's motives for coming over here. How quickly he remembered my friendship with Elise. The three-bedroom in Encino could just be an excuse to find out if I was going to the vigil at Carson Davis's estate. I could make the introductions to her family for him. My ex-husband, I remind myself, is the ultimate user.

I head upstairs to the bedroom where I hang the garment bag with my wedding dress in it in the very back of the walk-in closet, completely eclipsed by the crisp khaki trench coat my mother bought me over a year ago, with the *Lon-*

don Fog tags still on it. Hugh will never notice the dress, not that he's the nosy type to begin with. Though he may inquire whether I had any luck since I told him earlier today I'd be shopping for one. The thought of teasing him in the coming months about what it may or may not look like makes me smile.

I shut the closet door. Kyle is only just leaving. I hear the smooth sound of the Mercedes fading down the drive, but I restrain myself from looking out the window and catching the last stroke of chrome from the rear bumper. He makes things so goddamn hard for me. Every time I take an optimistic step towards my future with Hugh, my ex-husband finds a way to stay close behind.

Then I see it, that the dresser drawer where I keep my panties is slightly open. When I get closer I notice the colorful cotton bikini underwear I buy by the handful at Victoria's Secret are intermingled with the lace thongs I wear with my favorite pencil skirts or little black dresses. I am by no means a neat freak, but I'm not a slob either. I always close the drawers to my dresser whether I'm in a hurry or not, and I always separate the styles of my undergarments inside the drawer.

Who has been in here?

I think about Hugh rifling through there in order to know the right size to buy me some surprise sexy lingerie. But that's not his style. He wouldn't want me feeling pressured to wear it for him. He's the type who buys flowers, my favorite white gardenias, never in a box I will just throw out, but in a glass vase I can reuse for another time.

A burglar doesn't make any sense either because nothing downstairs was out of place or missing when Kyle and I came inside.

Kyle.

He'd been outside, sitting on the porch when I drove up, however it was possible he'd been in the house before I arrived. But what would be the point? He'd given me back his house key, took it clean off his key ring and handed it to me in front of two witnesses, his lawyer and mine. We were at my lawyer's office, a top floor spread downtown, during our one and only meeting to divide our assets. Everything had been so civil that my lawyer, a striking fifty-year-old woman with three law partners and no spouse, later commented after Kyle and his lawyer left that it was one of the easiest cases she'd ever dealt with.

On the divorce papers Kyle's hand doesn't look the same as when he'd signed our marriage certificate so many years before. Gone are the intentional flourishes of a young ambitious guy looking to make his mark. Instead the letters now run into one another, emphasizing agitation or impatience, a near middle-aged man caught up in his own indecisions.

Maybe Kyle *had* given me back his house key, but that didn't mean he hadn't made a copy. Because he was the one who left me, I'd never thought before now to change the locks.

CHAPTER ELEVEN

IN THE MORNING Hugh and I are still in bed, in that strange place where a couple senses the other is awake yet unwilling just yet to roll over, and admit it by facing each other. The curtains are closed, so the room has a gloomy feel, bulky shadows taking shape, like the straw hamper half-filled with unwashed clothes in the corner, my six drawer Maplewood dresser with the large, rectangle-shaped mirror hanging above it, or the half-open door that leads to the master bath. Last night Hugh and I had sex, taking our time, touching and kissing, a slow disrobing of me, then him. Then the intimate grind of trying for a baby.

In the dark of the bedroom I think about the unclosed dresser drawer I'd found, slightly cracked, several hours earlier, a possible intruder invading my space, someone's hands searching through my intimate items. Were they bare or did the person wear gloves? Was it hidden cash or jewelry this person was looking for or was it more personal? Am I blowing this out of proportion? Maybe I had left the dresser drawer open. I was running a little late picking up Jessica yesterday.

And there was no new note, not after the one

left under my car wiper the other afternoon. The sick prank, if that's what it is, most likely has ended. It's a relief not to be forced back into interpreting the connection between the hand and mind of a criminal.

No matter what Detective Ramirez may think of me, I don't want to be part of Elise's disappearance any more than I already am. I will be at the vigil this evening, but only because Kyle will be there and it will look bad if I don't go. Odds are he'll inform everyone he comes in contact with how Elise and I are longtime friends. While hand-in-hand with his new, unstable, most likely very fertile girlfriend he'll voice his curiosity about where I might be.

Our failed marriage will be the foundation for new real estate opportunities with all of Elise's wealthy friends and business associates.

I thought you'd be done with your ex by now, Becca, that frizzy-haired slut had said to Kyle, but she was unmistakably looking right at me. Was she really a slut or was I putting that on her because she was involved with my ex-husband? She had to be more than an easy lay to make it to a good graduate school like the one she was in at UCLA. She had to be pretty damn smart.

My mind can't help going there. Seeing the two of them acting like they belong *at my friend's vigil*. Seeing the two of them naked, out of breath, their limbs tangled up in each other in bed as if rough sex is somehow the same as real passion. Is she using protection or is she planning on trapping him by getting pregnant? Would he even feel trapped if it was an "accident"? Laney told me how easy it was to simply slip up with contraception. I had to be honest and up front about it all and wind up divorced. Some might call it ironic if Kyle were to become a father after leaving me for wanting to have a child. I'll simply call it devastating.

What is the point of holding a vigil anyway other than it serving as a precursor to the tragic news Elise is indeed dead? Do we really need to stand elbow-to-elbow and weep and pray for her with obligatory lit candles in hand poking through the center of paper plates?

There is the real possibility Elise really is alright and it simply hit her in the driveway that afternoon, her father's life on the verge of ending while a new life is in the making inside her wife Deborah. And Elise drove off to clear her head, to process it all, dropping her shoe in her rush to get away from the pregnant woman who was the source of her happy future.

Elise was never the same after losing her mother at such a young age, a year after I'd lost my father. It was, after all, a death that could've been prevented, a death of vice and bad choices. We were thirteen and I was around to see what she did with her grief, how she balled it up like an unused tissue and crammed it in her coat pocket. When I lost my father, it was different, more like a cruel act of God than anything my mother, sister, or I could've stopped. My father owned two tire shops, one in Orange County, the other in Burbank, and had been healthy, energetic, still helping his employees when things got busy, changing out worn thirty to fifty-pound pick-up truck treads for brand new ones. Mrs. Davis had a choice. My father died in his sleep without getting one.

Later, after my sister Laney began smiling again, it frustrated me, how our father became a fond memory for her, a person she spoke of in conversation without tearing up. I couldn't talk about him or the silent affliction that burst that night through the most crucial vessel in his head, killing him while the rest of us slept. Unlike those lucky people who find closure, the thought of losing him has remained too fresh. His death mixes me up in ways I've learned to keep to myself so I don't face my sister's critical concern for my wellbeing.

Even if it doesn't always feel that way, *my life is on track*. Hugh and I *are* moving forward. The dress I'm marrying him in is only feet away, hanging in my closet. Soon I'll work on the rest of the arrangements to plan the wedding.

On the nightstand I hear my phone going off, indicating a new text message. Hugh groans.

"Why'd you bring that thing up here?"

Why did I take it with me last night?

Because my house is so remote, set deep back at the end of the road, surrounded by trees, my property butting up to hills that extend even further out, cell reception is unpredictable. Usually I only bring up the cordless phone connected to the landline if Hugh is staying at his place in Santa Monica and we talk a while before saying goodnight. There are a lot of reasons why I absentmindedly brought my cell with me, work, news about Elise – I was scared. But did I really have any reason to be? Hugh is here and the notes have stopped.

The ring for the same unanswered text message goes off again.

Before I have a chance to roll over and silence my phone, Hugh gently grabs me. His muscular arm, with the visible white tan line from the short sleeve t-shirts he wears to the construction site, blocks me. Then he draws me closer to the middle of the bed, to the heat of his body.

I smell the salty ocean of the Malibu site where he spends most of his time in his hair.

"No," he whispers against my cheek, "I'm not done having my way with you just yet."

Outside I hear soft rain, the reason why Hugh is still in bed with me and not getting ready for work. In this moment he and I are making a new memory, a cozy warm one of our two bodies close together under a down comforter that I'll remember when I'm idling in traffic or stirring vegetables in the skillet for dinner.

Relationships consist of strand after strand of memories, a stored history linking two people. Hugh and I are just getting started. Sometimes that thought exhausts me while other times, like now, it excites me.

With one arm still around me, he lifts the back of my hair, flicking his tongue against my neck. I lower my hand into the covers, reaching inside his boxers, feeling he's clearly up for morning sex.

My phone makes the same noise.

Instead of pulling away and shutting it off, I turn towards my fiancé. The sporadic interruptions from my phone will annoy me, but it won't bother Hugh and I've learned, when it comes to the man I'm with wanting to make love to me, it's sometimes less complicated if I just give in.

It isn't until Hugh heads into the bathroom to shower that I check my phone. The text is from Kyle.

Have you seen this?

Beside the text is a live link and when I click on it, a small vessel appears, bobbing in the ocean on its side, a million-dollar sailboat almost looking like a cheap toy. The capsized boat pans in and out of focus, growing in size, taking the shape of a much larger sailboat, the kind with a spacious cabin beneath. It's been found two miles out of the calm waters of Vigo Bay where the water opens out to the rough and cold Atlantic Ocean.

A news helicopter hovers above the wreckage. Down below, in the center of the halo the whirring blades create, floats a couch cushion and what appears to be a cutting board used to gut the fish plucked live out of the water.

Under the footage is the caption: BOATING ACCIDENT – ACTOR CARSON DAVIS MISSING.

I sit up in bed. Three search boats flank the scene in hopes of finding the sole survivor. Rescue divers in bright red scuba gear drop into the choppy water.

But they will find no body, this I know. Why would the family go to such lengths to stage Carson's death? Why not let him die in a hospital bed, *the way I saw him*, just a few days ago? No one will believe me if I tell what I know, *what I saw.*

Deborah will obviously deny it, and I will look like the delusional one. Detective Ramirez already thinks I'm making the notes up. My own fiancé might even tell me I could be mistaken.

After all, there is the physical evidence of a capsized boat off the coast of Spain to consider, with a missing helmsman. The twenty-four-hour news cycle that will continue to play this out, hour after hour. This footage will butt into his daughter's vigil later today. A body lost at sea makes for good drama. No doubt there will be at least one witness, a housekeeper or local who'll claim he or she saw Carson go out on the boat the day before.

Had this plan been in the works long before I appraised his estate in Bel Air or is this improvised? Does it have anything to do with my showing up at Gia's store yesterday?

"Jesus, Tia. What is it?"

Hugh fills the doorframe, fresh from the shower, a towel knotted at his waist.

"Your face is white."

"Nothing." I turn off the phone. "Just checking the time of the vigil for Elise this evening."

The light from the bathroom casts on the water droplets still on his shoulder blades, and as he passes me into the bedroom to get dressed, I notice something on the back of his upper arm. Hugh blames all of his minor injuries on work.

A scab, a few days old, that looks like it came from the fierce drag of a woman's nail. Mine are clipped short.

CHAPTER TWELVE

THE TRAIL OF parked cars begins several blocks away letting me know I'm on the right route to the Davis Estate. The vehicles range from a shiny black SUV Porsche Carrera to a Honda Accord and an old gray Subaru with political stickers, some even so far back as from the Clinton-Gore era, tagging the entire rear bumper. Word about the vigil must've gone public through the news, viral soon after, trending on social media sites.

I just assumed Kyle had heard about it through our real estate contacts, a primarily closed clique of gossips. The Elise I knew when we were younger wouldn't want such an orchestrated fuss about her disappearance. Why are you all standing around crying? Why aren't you people looking for me? she'd say.

"Maybe we should take another street, park and walk the rest of the way."

I'd almost forgotten Hugh was in the passenger seat. He's been so quiet or I've been too distracted by Elise and the thought of having to be civil to Kyle and his basket-case girlfriend. Out of nowhere that long hairline-scratch I'd seen across

Hugh's back when he came out of the shower pops into my head.

Why must my mind immediately go to assuming the worst? Is it because what Kyle said holds some truth, that deep down I fear I don't really know my fiancé very well? Is it possible some other woman accidentally got carried away when they were in bed together? The mark so slight even Hugh didn't notice?

There are nights when he stays at his apartment in Santa Monica, and he could easily call me on his cell from another woman's bedroom. He is friends with Glen, the sleaziest man in all of real estate with a sketchy background no one can seem to nail down.

I don't want to doubt Hugh's love for me, yet here I am trying to poke holes into the most solid relationship with a man I've ever had.

It's just a scratch, the kind Hugh could've gotten anywhere on the construction site where there are exposed beams and jutting nails.

Insecurity, if you let it wound you, rarely heals.

"Hey, Tia…"

I've been too silent in the car and my fiancé has picked up on it.

"I think she might be dead," I blurt out.

I've startled him. I sense Hugh staring at me yet I keep my eyes on the road.

"Why are you so sure?"

The truth hits me hard, the knowledge I hold from having worked with police on other missing persons cases in the past.

"The Davis Family would be holed up with

the police, getting the money together, if it was a ransom kidnapping. Instead they're having this very public vigil."

I brake abruptly.

A series of orange cones have been lined up indicating two different lanes I may drive down and park.

I follow a cop in an orange vest that is directing me with his flashlight towards one of the lanes. I do my best to give myself extra space between the car in front of me in the hopes we may get out of here, though I doubt that will be an option.

I imagine by the end of the hour this entire private road will be lined up with cars worse than the chaos outside of the Hollywood Bowl for a sold out concert. When we get out of the car it almost feels like we're going to an entertainment event, not a somber vigil for a woman who, as a celebrity's child, has done her best to stay out of the public eye.

Hugh takes my hand and we follow the flow of people towards the Davis estate.

At the front gates a newswoman interviews a man and woman who look like they're some-where in their sixties, wearing matching white t-shirts with a black silhouette of Carson Davis's face, his slash of strong chin and swipe for his full head of silver hair. The man is doing most of the talking while the woman hunches into his chest. A white handkerchief flits in front of her face and her sobs sound genuine.

Carson Davis is an American icon like Elvis, Frank Sinatra or Jack Nicholson. Real fame, the kind one can't undo, means by becoming a recluse in his last years made him just as popular as if he'd shown his face at every movie premier for the last five years. Avoiding the public for so long also obscures the timeline when he first became so gravely ill.

A lightweight brunette in a hoodie, jeans and sneakers, gets to her feet on the hood of a white sedan. A bullhorn is held to her lips because she's about to cause a scene.

"Pray for this family," she implores to those few people who've stopped to hear what she has to say and to the others who walk right past her. "We, at the Carson Davis fan club, know what he'd want us to do at this time." She holds up her fist as if at a rally energizing an important social movement.

The other fans who've gathered at the front bumper hold up their fists back to her.

"Tougher than the hardest punch," someone yells.

It's a famous line from one of Carson's films where he plays an old retired fighter suffering with Parkinson's. He was the kind of versatile actor who could seamlessly star in a musical one year and a drama the next.

"Jesus," Hugh mumbles. "What a goddamn circus."

I agree, though I say nothing.

So much for this vigil being for Elise. Is that the point of staging Carson Davis's so-called accident? To obscure Elise's kidnapping? Has this been someone's plan all along? Who else in the family knew about Carson's condition besides Elise and Deborah? Lit candles poking through paper plates are being handed out, creating an eerie, hopeless glow in the crowd as if we are all mourning Elise's passing, not praying for her safe return.

Just a few yards, deep into the front lawn, stands a makeshift stage, the kind with two fold-out metal steps you might see at an outside elementary school awards assembly or a mall opening with the local mayor. This marks the cut-off point for the crowd, well before the mansion even is in view. Actual cops with guns and no doubt zip ties should anyone pose a threat, flank both sides of the stage.

Hugh and I stand off to the edge of the crowd, midway to the stage. Thankfully the mood is darker here, more appropriate considering the circumstances. Most of the gatherers are quiet, holding the candles, others are using the light from their phones.

Among us lurks the person or persons responsible for abducting Elise. There is little doubt. Most of them enjoy either coming back to the scene, observing their bloody handiwork behind the police caution tape or standing side by side at a public vigil, getting a charge listening to the cries and prayers from the friends and the loved ones of their victim.

Their victim.

For them, it's oddly personal. For them, our suffering is the ultimate power.

I feel a sudden swell of nausea and I look up

towards the clear night sky for a breath of fresh air. How I wish this is a physical symptom of pregnancy and not the brutal knowledge that my childhood friend is most likely dead. The police just haven't found her body yet. I've worked too many cases to hold on to much hope.

Hugh squeezes my hand.

"Tia? You okay?"

I return the pressure, yet I don't look away from the sky, the smattering of stars, the sight of a news helicopter closing in from the north.

I take another deep breath before I force myself to focus on Hugh, and I kiss his stubbly cheek. I'm lucky to have found someone who is so attentive to me. He'd leave the vigil right now, no questions, if I asked him to.

An attractive man cuts through the crowd, coming straight towards us. He's in his late thirties with curly light brown hair, blue eyes. Elise's eyes, then I remember. It's Edward, her slightly older brother, the one that was sent off to boarding school in Maryland somewhere to the kind of highbrow institution that turns out senators and congressmen. Carson Davis wanted more for his son than what Hollywood had to offer.

One time during his freshman year, when he was home on a visit, he kissed me in the dark of the kitchen pantry in the Davis home. I was twelve, my dad had died a little under six months before. I'd just turned out the light and was about to head into the kitchen, but Edward slipped in front of me and closed the door.

It wasn't a pushy kiss, not one where he tried

to get his tongue in my mouth or feel me up. It was a long close-mouthed kiss. His hands held either side of my face as if he knew even at his age then that he had to be gentle with someone like me. I felt myself drop the bag of tortilla chips I'd gone into the pantry to retrieve. I remember kissing him back even though I hardly knew him, practical strangers linked by our closeness to one person, his sister. Somehow that connection alone made it seem like our lips softly pressed together was okay.

I remember how I felt that kiss everywhere as if it somehow consumed me. I remember sliding my arms around his waist that had been as skinny as mine.

Then he was gone before I could flip on the light and pick up the bag off the floor. When I came into Elise's bedroom with the chips she smiled sneakily and asked if I liked making out with her brother. I felt my face color with shame. She was lying on her stomach, head first at the foot of the bed, a magazine unfolded in front of her. "I dared Edward this morning to be your first kiss. He told me a while back he thinks you're cute."

"Tia…" Edward says to me now, hesitating as if he must carefully choose his words, "it's good to see you again."

I lean in as he kisses my cheek. I wonder what level of fear he's keeping in about his sister being missing. While Edward had spent so much time away at school I know he and Elise were of like minds, jointly figuring how to play on my innocence that night in the kitchen pantry. Some siblings don't have to work at being close like Laney and me so often do.

Edward pulls back so he may look at me head on.

"This must be hard on you too since I heard you're one of the last people to see her before she disappeared."

Why does that sound, however subtle coming from him, as if he's implicating me of something?

I nod because there is nothing else I can do.

"Edward," he says turning to Hugh, shaking his hand. Of course, it doesn't cross my mind to introduce the two of them. It's a polite exchange of pleasantries between Edward and my fiancé, but it's also a way for Edward to put Hugh at ease.

I'm surprised his face, so youthful and smooth, bears no signs of braving the altitude, the freezing temperatures and bone-chilling wind of a place like Nepal.

Elise's brother turns his attention back to me.

"I was hoping you and I could meet for coffee or lunch tomorrow. In part to catch up, but I also have a few questions."

He looks towards the empty stage as if expecting someone to suddenly appear.

An enlarged photo of Elise is propped up on an easel. Her smile is real and her blond hair shiny under the light of the photographer's flash. She looks like she's dressed for a wedding, the neckline of her dark pink suit is visible. Maybe it's her own.

"Sure," I say to her brother. "But I don't know

how much help…"

"Tia, there's…" Edward interrupts, looking directly at me before he smiles like he catches himself being too aggressive. "I mean, I'd just like to hear what you know."

Gia comes out on the stage in a tight black knee length dress and the kind of ice pick heels only supermodels and strippers can balance on. Next to her is an older man in an expensive suit and a neatly trimmed gray beard. Definitely not a sibling of Carson's. He was an only child. The Davis lawyer, maybe? Given the status of Gia's marriage with Carson, I hadn't thought I'd see her playing such a prominent role at the vigil. If Gia hasn't told Edward about me showing up at her store yesterday, she definitely will now.

Edward shakes hands again with Hugh, a sign of sorts between men that Hugh has nothing to worry about. A romance is not why he wants to meet me alone.

"Great," Edward says to me as he walks away. "Noon at the Polo Lounge." He's picked an exclusive restaurant, a practical landmark for tourists and therefore easy for me to find.

He climbs the two steps to the stage in one easy stride.

When he stands next to Gia, the two of them look more like a couple than stepmother and stepson. That is the culture these days where family members don't always make sense, where age matters, oftentimes more than love, and women have an expiration date while men of means or celebrity simply do not.

Edward draws the crowd into silence, not like a man who has just come from hiking twenty thousand feet up in the Himalayan Mountains helping the poverty stricken, but like Carson Davis's son, a confident man about to put a stop to a spiraling situation.

Across the other side of the stage I see her, the fake white blonde of her hair, the way she tucks it behind one ear once she sees me too. Has the sight of me somehow put her on edge? She clutches onto his arm, the arm of my ex-husband. What the hell are they really doing at my friend's vigil? Then it occurs to me that maybe she doesn't want to be here. Kyle used to spring plans on me after I was securely belted in the passenger seat, clueless as to what he had in store for us.

Kyle doesn't detect her sudden touch. He doesn't realize she appears infuriated enough to shout at me and make a scene in front of so many people. I wonder what he's told her, if he's dumb enough to share fond memories of our married life to a woman with a restraining order against her.

Typical of my ex-husband, he's too busy scrolling through email on his phone, a new listing he might've missed or a client he feels compelled to respond to.

Becca whispers in his ear, her eyes still on me.

He nods, but doesn't look up at her.

Am I smiling? Because she quickly looks away from me, humiliated and livid, a combination she doesn't wear well.

I could've warned her Kyle always puts the woman in his life second to his career ambitions of being a prominent professor in his field at UCLA and a real estate agent to the wealthy. He's here for selfish purposes, to pass out his business card to the right people, ensure the right first impression.

Edward has been speaking this entire time I've been having a stare down with Becca.

"And while this night is supposed to be strictly about my dear sister." Edward waits a beat. "Just over an hour ago…they recovered my father's body."

I look up towards the man I haven't seen in over two decades. In many ways Edward is a stranger. I only vaguely knew the teenage boy. He says this last part about his father so matter-of-factly that even I nearly think it's true.

So Carson Davis is in fact dead.

The last time I saw him, he was breathing on a respirator, but he was still very much alive.

This is how the charade ends, with one hell of a cinematic story that includes a foreign country, a sailboat and a search party. Actors will be lining up to play the part for this is not a story about faking one's death which many people have been guilty of attempting to do, some even proving successful in doing so. It's about faking the manner in which you died – too distraught from the news of his daughter gone missing expert sailor Carson Davis fails to right the sail in treacherous waters and drowns.

Maybe the family is simply following Carson's

wishes. Maybe instead of a well-planned funeral, he came up with an elaborate way in which he'd be found dead, a death suitable for Hollywood royalty of the adventurous sort like Steve McQueen or John Wayne. Carson isn't the first celebrity to hide his dire medical condition from the public. Well known figures have gone to great lengths to keep their personal ailments private. For years President Reagan successfully hid his Alzheimer's diagnosis somehow even when he was in the company of others. Recently a prominent director suddenly died from cancer that virtually nobody even knew he suffered from.

Sharp cries change the tenor of the vigil and I wonder how the woman who stood on the car with the bullhorn or the couple giving the interview are holding up at the news. They seem like the kind of fans who think of Carson as if he's a family member which doesn't necessarily make them full-blown fanatics. His films may have more than entertained them. Maybe his films brought these people happiness during impossibly dark times in their lives.

Gia grabs Edward's hand and together they face the crowd, a united front, patiently waiting for the wave of emotion to subside. The older man with the beard is still standing with them, but his hands are at his sides as if he's served his purpose and there's no need for him onstage anymore.

Something is wrong with this picture. Deborah is missing from the stage. *She* should be up there talking about her wife Elise, breathing life into an investigation that might soon grow cold. The media will lose interest. For at least the next several days Carson's death will overshadow Elise's disappearance. His funeral, the footage of his films, snippets of his most memorable interviews, all of it will be more important than what's happened to his daughter.

"We want to thank the recovery team in Spain," Edward continues.

I've stopped hearing the rest of what he's saying because I've finally spotted Deborah. She's standing half-hidden between the little stage and the sickly white trunk of a sycamore tree. Beside her is Detective Ramirez and briefly they glance my way before returning to what looks like an intense back and forth exchange.

Is Deborah telling him how I came by her house the other day with the appraisal papers? That I was fishing around, asking questions about the investigation? Or has she already told him much more like how far back my relationship with her wife goes – how one might argue in one senseless snap decision it has turned friendship into the kind of entanglement neither Elise or I have ever truly broken free from?

She has something on me and I have something on her.

Over the years of intimacy with Deborah, maybe Elise shared with her what had happened that afternoon when we were alone with Elise's mother at the beach house in Malibu, ugly details I've managed to keep from my family, Kyle and Hugh. Here I am standing under the night sky at her vigil. The woman could be alive or dead and

I realize Elise has done it to me again, coerced me into keeping yet another piece of vital knowledge about the fate of one of her parents.

I will forever be her gutless, unwitting accomplice.

Not far from where I am, Deborah might be getting things all wrong with the detective. She might be pointing out to him that by me being one of the last known persons to see Elise the day she disappeared, I might be much more than a witness. I might be a suspect.

CHAPTER THIRTEEN

AFTER THE VIGIL, once back at home, Hugh and I do not try for a baby. That monthly window of opportunity, during these seven to ten days while I'm ovulating is gradually closing. Soon I'll get the blood red reminder of my period, a biological warning of sorts that time is running out for me to become a mother. Another vital egg shed from my uterus. Even though the doctor has reassured me, I still can't help but worry that all those years I took the pill while married to Kyle somehow screwed up my hormones. Maybe deep inside me, my body *thinks* I don't want a new life taking form in here.

Tonight, neither Hugh or I feel in the mood for sex and Hugh, especially Hugh, can't get over how tragic it all is – an elderly father suddenly losing his own life shortly after finding out about his daughter's disappearance. Most likely he is thinking about his own daughter, how she inexplicably lost her mother, in her teens, when she needed her most. His daughter is the one who'd come home from school and found her mother, face down, floating in the shallow end of the pool. She'd been the one who dialed 911, then had to wait with a neighbor more than two hours before her father could get home to her from his job site in Santa Barbara. When Hugh finally told me what happened to his late wife, he'd covered his face with his hands, "It's those two goddamn hours that I can never make up to my daughter. How alone she must've felt, at the worst time in her life, without either of her parents."

Hugh is quiet as he systematically goes around the house in his sweatpants and white V-neck t-shirt, locking up. The vigil has taken a lot out of him. Someone else's grief always reminds us of our own.

I head up to bed.

I say nothing to challenge what Edward told my fiancé and the rest of the crowd because in this case the truth is more implausible than the lie. Carson taking out the boat to clear his head after learning the news about his only daughter made perfect sense. He had always been an avid sailor. He loved the water and felt an attachment to it which was why the house he shared when he was married to Elise's mother had been perched on a cliff right off PCH in Malibu. After her death he sold it because of the terrible memories, though he shortly thereafter purchased the coastal vacation home in Spain. Could it even be possible that Gia is not in on the Carson Davis charade and that she, too, has been duped into believing that he was of sound mind, working on his memoir in Spain and not being artificially kept alive in the same city where she lives? But then why tell me their marriage is strong when

Deborah had said the two of them were in the process of a divorce?

Am I lying to my fiancé by withholding what I know about Carson being on the ventilator only a few days ago? It feels as if I am, that I must tell somebody. Hugh will want to believe me and will do his best to try. But maybe he'll think I'm getting things all mixed up, or like the detective intimated about the notes, that I'm making things up.

As Hugh's heavy footsteps creak louder up the stairs, my anxiety builds. Instinctively, I roll on to my side, facing the wall. The pressure to come clean with what I know about Carson's death will pass if I just pretend I'm already asleep.

I'm five minutes early, but Elise's brother is already here seated at a roomy circular booth in the back of the busy restaurant. Maybe he's chosen it for privacy, but I'm made aware of his wealth, how much extra space it can buy in a crowded restaurant even during the peak lunch hour.

A clean-shaven guy in his twenties turns away from the table as I approach. At first, I assume he's a waiter except he's in a white button down shirt and faded jeans with an expensive leather book bag on one shoulder. We smile at each other as he passes, though I notice the helpless way he glances back, sizing me up like I'm an important detail he forgot to include in his notes. But it appears he thinks better of returning to ask me my name and instead rushes out the door.

"A reporter from the *Times*," Edward says, extending his arm towards the opposite side of the booth where I am to take a seat.

A waitress whisks by to drop off an icy glass of water as well as a menu for me. This is the type of fancy understated place where the help anticipates your needs – you rarely need to ask.

Edward looks disheveled like he hasn't slept, his eyes bloodshot. Jet lag, a dead father and a missing sister might've obviously kept him up last night. An empty imported beer and a glass, nearly finished, sit in front of him.

The polished representative of the Davis Family I heard speak last night is showing some wear.

"I'm offering a one hundred thousand dollars reward for information on Elise." Edward shrugs, then glances in the direction of the reporter who's already left. "Claims he'll put it below the fold on the front cover of the paper, seeing I gave him the exclusive. He'd better not be bullshitting me."

The way Elise's brother says this last part makes it sound like a threat he'll definitely carry out. Under the restaurant lights I notice his pinkie nail is gone and there is a tattoo, in another language I can't figure out, on the tender part of his wrist. He may be a celebrity's son, but he's apparently spent most of his adult life in another country, in a much higher altitude, climbing as far away from it as he can.

I sit down, take a drink of water and attempt to relax.

"No one's called about a ransom?"

Edward picks up on my surprise, then shakes his head. He drains the rest of his glass of beer.

"Nothing yet, though the cops tell us not to rule it out."

Us.

I wonder if he's strictly referring to Gia and the bearded man or if Deborah is also included.

"Whoever might've taken her, if that's what this is, could wait a week or more so we sweat it out. Then place the call when we're desperate and about to give up hope. We'll be weaker that way and likely to give them everything they want."

The same waitress from before stops at the table, switches out Edward's empty bottle and glass with a fresh round. She waits, assuming I'm ready to order, and I flip open the menu and decide within seconds on a salmon salad with the house dressing. The sooner I can get this meal with Elise's brother over with the better.

He's making me nervous, watching me in a singular way he couldn't have at the crowded vigil, which I realize now is the very reason why he asked for us to meet privately.

As one of the last known persons to see Elise before her disappearance, I should expect her brother's questions. After observing the detective and Deborah last night actively discussing something, maybe discussing me, I can't help but feel a little paranoid.

"What do you mean *if that's what this is*?" I say. "What else could've happened?"

I realize how horribly insensitive my questions are, but I've blurted them out and there's no way

I can take them back. If someone hasn't kidnapped Elise for money, then they must've killed her for revenge. My second question doesn't need answering.

"Deborah is still under the assumption Elise might've gotten spooked about something and left on her own."

The way he says her name makes it clear he doesn't think much of his sister-in-law or her theory of what happened to his sibling.

"If someone's taken her, the detectives think Elise might know the person."

Edward leans back as if there's no need to move forward and put the pressure on me. In his own way, he already is. He can tell there's something I'm keeping from him. He knows because his sister must've told him all about me, my insecurities, the way I weaken when I feel cornered. Sitting here with me now, it's probably all coming back to him. That night in the pantry my mouth hadn't just met Edward's, it'd met Elise's too. They'd shared me the way they shared everything between them.

"I'm sorry about your father."

I abruptly change the subject. It's what I always do when afraid of confrontation. It's what I did with Kyle. It took him three tries before he told me for certain he was not interested in ever becoming a father.

If Elise's brother is somehow estranged from Deborah, now is the time to inform him of what I know, how Spain is a grand scheme. Because he was in Nepal, he might not have had any idea his father had actually been dying in his own home in Bel Air. Nobody except Elise and Deborah and the medical team responsible for the equipment know for certain how long Carson had been on that respirator.

Someone, at least Elise's wife, has been lying. Elise has been too. The two of them could've been in some type of conspiracy, to what, prevent Edward and any others from access to Carson before his death? Could they have altered his will or destroyed a new one in order to rely on an older one with the right beneficiaries?

I want to say something. I clear my throat, just so I may hear the sound of my own voice, that I'm physically capable of coming out with the truth, if I can only find the right words.

The waitress returns to the table with my salad, and I take one bite, then another.

The silence between us is filled with the loud restaurant sounds of plural conversations and dinnerware clinking.

"I understand you haven't seen Elise in some time, years in fact. Not until the other day when you appraised my father's house. You two used to be so close."

He takes a full swallow of his beer that he hasn't bothered this time to pour into the empty glass. The way he's staring makes it seem like he already knows the answers to the questions he's asking. But he wants to hear them from me anyway.

"How did you get the job again, if you weren't in contact with each other? She keeps appraisers on the payroll. Why you?"

"I don't know." I sound defensive which does little to convince Edward to stop coming after me. If he thinks I'd ever hurt his sister or set her up in some way to be kidnapped, he couldn't be more wrong. *They* were the type of people capable of manipulating situations to suit their own ends, *not me.* "She got in touch with me, not the other way around."

Edward seems unwilling to let it go.

"For some reason I thought the two of you had had a falling out."

The image of a young Elise standing before her mother's coffin that had made the local news comes to mind. Her blonde hair, long and straight at the time, fell forward, obscuring what grief must've shown on her face. It had been a closed casket because the injuries to Elise's mother had been too severe.

I shake my head, regretting I'd ever agreed to this lunch. There were plenty of reasons why I distanced myself from his sister and Edward knew it. *He knew her* considering he was so much like her. He was just better at hiding that part of himself with his generous acts in an impoverished region of the world.

"We just lost touch with each other," I say, sticking to my story no matter how false it may sound.

Edward's phone goes off on the table, but he silences it without checking to see who called.

"Well," he says, his voice different, as if he's grown frustrated I've told him nothing about his sister's disappearance than he already knows.

"What a coincidence that you've had the misfortune of being present for the two worst tragedies my family has ever endured."

His words hit like cement blocks, one hurled at my chest after the other, and I do my best not to show it. I force myself to take in some water, then another forkful of salad before I excuse myself to the restroom.

Once inside the women's bathroom, I lock myself inside one of the two stalls. I take a shallow breath, then a deeper one. So Elise *had* confided in her brother about the day her mother drove off drunk, crazed with heartache and crashed head on to another car on Pacific Coast Highway, killing herself and a forty-two year old pediatrician who had a wife and three young children.

For some stupid reason I assumed it was the one thing she would never tell Edward because it had been his mother too.

Elise and I were in the family room watching a comedy when her mother's cry ripped right through the volume of the TV.

Something someone said on the other end of the line clearly upset her. "You say his car is parked out there right now?" Her voice was shaky, a rough mix of anguish and alcohol, and as a young teen I felt the instability of the only adult in the house losing control while her daughter Elise chose to block it out by turning up the sound.

I felt my chest burn with fear of what Mrs. Davis might be capable of doing next.

Then I caught a glimpse of the woman, her untucked blouse and white jeans that had some type of dark stain on them, maybe red wine, as she made her way into the kitchen for something far stronger. There wasn't a time when I came over that she didn't have a tumbler of liquor in her hand, usually vodka and there was always a bright slice of lime in it and the ritzy sounding clink of ice cubes. On nice clear days she would usually take it outside to the pool, inhale the ocean air and recline on a chaise lounge in a fashionable floppy hat and a sleek black one piece.

That day, that moment when she interrupted our movie, was different. Mrs. Davis had heard the kind of news that just altered her life. She was grieving in that undone way my mother had when I overheard her crying late one night shortly after my father passed. Unlike my mother who pulled herself together by the morning, I only saw Mrs. Davis emotionally unraveling even more.

"I don't care if that old son of a bitch fucks his fans," she muttered. "It's *this one bitch* I care about. You said she lives less than five fucking miles from our own goddamn house?"

I turned to Elise, the cut of her profile, as she kept her eyes on the TV screen.

"Shouldn't we try and talk to your mom? She sounds pretty mad."

At thirteen we weren't so young that we couldn't have done something to distract her from her rage, at least maybe get her off the phone with the person who was clearly only fueling it.

Elise finally looked at me, practically bored by my concern over her mother's theatrics.

Before she answered, something broke hard on the tile floor of the foyer, solid glass that shattered from the force of being thrown. I thought of the International Film Award Carson Davis kept under special track lighting on the mantle in the living room. There would be no turning back for Mrs. Davis now.

What came next lasted less than a minute, though it seemed so much longer as she wildly searched room to room for her car keys, then burst out the front door without her purse and no shoes on her feet. Elise and I watched from the front room window as her mother peeled out of the circular driveway in a white Ranger Rover, swerving wide to avoid running down an elderly couple out walking their cocker spaniel.

As I stand here in the restroom stall old guilt ignites inside me all over again at *what I didn't do* that day. I knew then as I do now that by allowing a woman who was dangerously under the influence and certainly out of her mind leave the house and get behind the wheel of a car, I am an accessory to her death. I am an accessory to the death of an innocent man, a father, with a family waiting for him at home whom she also killed. I'd lost my own father just one year before, and I understood only too well the pain that man's children would always feel.

Being thirteen or thirty-five, the blood of two people is still very much on my hands.

I hear the door to the women's restroom open

yet the person doesn't get into the stall next to me nor does that person wash her hands. She lingers, probably checking her hair and make-up in the mirror because it's suddenly grown silent.

With my sleeve, I wipe my eyes because I don't want Edward to see that his harsh comment, how I've been around for the two worst things that could ever happen to his family, really did a number on me.

For years I've told myself there was nothing I could've done yet my actions that day or rather the lack of them make me no different than the cruel teenagers I recently saw on the news. They joked and pointed at the man in the deep center of a pond while filming him flailing for his life, then posted the drowning on social media sites.

If Hugh ever finds out, he'll insist I was young and overwhelmed by the entire situation. Though he'll make the right excuses for me, a part of him will think less of me, this I know.

After the police arrived later that day with Carson, Elise fell into her father's arms, sobbing. Over his shoulder she locked eyes with me, eyes without any tears in them.

"We had no idea Mom had even left," she cried into his chest. "We were in the backyard sitting on the diving board eating popsicles."

I unlatch the stall door because I don't know how long I've been gone from the table. Edward is probably wondering what is keeping me.

When I step out I see I'm alone in the bathroom.

A yellow Post-it note is stuck to the mirror,

the kind big enough to list a couple of errands to run. Except, as I step closer, I see there is only one word written in red ballpoint, in a childlike scrawl. The message in the center is as startling as a fresh cut wound.

CHAPTER FOURTEEN

MY HEART IS beating so rapidly I have no clue how to slow it down. Unlike the other two notes, there is no doubt this one is left for me. The childlike scrawl of the note is not someone faking a kid's writing. No. The slant of the lettering, the near perfect "u" means the writer most likely is a right hander and has written with their left in order to disguise their distinct style.

Whoever put it here boldly entered the restroom, betting I was still in a stall or maybe at this point it doesn't matter because she could care less.

It is a *she*. I am now almost sure of it.

I think of Kyle's unstable girlfriend, the razor-sharp way she focused on me last night at the vigil. Would she track me here? She has at least one restraining order against her. Kyle made it sound like she just loved too hard in her last relationship and the court order is some kind of badge of honor she's earned.

I don't know how she harassed her ex. Maybe it had been through writing cryptic or threatening notes.

Kyle must've told her in the past I'd been a

handwriting analyst and she relished in this being the perfect way to get back at me. But why would she do it? She already has my ex-husband. We are divorced and I am engaged to another man.

Quickly, before another woman enters, I take a white paper towel from the dispensary and use it to pluck the note from the glass.

There is the possibility Detective Ramirez will definitely check this note for fingerprints. The other two I've given him have probably been completely disregarded, taking up space somewhere in his desk drawer along with pens, notepads and paperclips.

I no longer see the notes as necessarily being related to Elise's disappearance. If Becca has been stalking me, she obviously knew I'd been with Elise Davis.

She must've seen me with her.

The fact Elise has gone missing and it's all over the news is a timely coincidence that factored in well with plans already set in place.

That psycho bitch.

A woman in her fifties with dyed red hair and a smart white pantsuit smiles politely at the open door. Upon seeing my expression, she appears uncomfortable, rushing right past me into a stall.

I must've looked crazed. I feel crazed.

The former analyst in me can't stop thinking.

Most people are right handed.

I am right handed.

More than three quarters of the world is right handed, so this is not much of a clue I've come up with. But at least it's something I can tell the police.

Back at the booth, Edward is signing the bill. Although his signature from where I'm standing is upside down, I spot the heavy pressure of his hand, a sign of restrained aggression.

He looks up at me, as I approach, almost like he's expecting somebody else. This is the second person I've just startled.

"What's the matter, Tia?"

His expression has drastically changed. He looks worried as if he has to handle me carefully and I remember the boy in the dark of the pantry who instinctively thought to cradle my face in his warm hands before his lips touched mine.

"I apologize if I…"

"This was left for me in the bathroom," I say, cutting him off. I unfold the top part of the paper towel, so Edward can see the messily written word and the exclamation point, the red ink and yellow paper under the bright light of the restaurant.

To Edward, it might not seem like much. The twisted minds of the people who write these kinds of notes taunt the receiver more than anybody else, like a stalker who breathes on the other end of the line, then hangs up, never saying a word and spooks their target into being fearful of what will happen next. And this time, this third note works – the words pour out of me. I decide to tell Edward everything.

"I've found two other notes a couple days ago. They appeared shortly after Elise went missing."

I sit back down at my place in the booth. My

salad is still on the table, which almost doesn't make sense anymore since I've long since lost my appetite.

"I wanted to believe it was just a prank. The first one was put partway under my front door-mat, but then the second one I found beneath the wiper of my car after I'd appraised a property."

Edward crosses his arms at his chest, slowly taking in what I've said. He's a man who hikes for hours on end, then camps for the night in life threatening weather conditions. I doubt he ever makes a snap decision.

"Why do you think they have anything to do with my sister?"

"They might not."

I decide not to reveal my suspicions that my ex-husband's girlfriend is behind the notes because I'm already overwhelming Edward enough by telling him about them in the first place. By the stunned expression on his face it's pretty clear he knows nothing about the other two notes. Either that or he is as good of an actor as his late father.

"But one of them," I say, "read *Are you hopeful she is still alive?* I gave them to the detective earlier this week when he came by my house. But then this one was left in the bathroom just now."

My eyes quickly search the room for a full account of all the other customers enjoying their lunches in the packed restaurant. Their profiles, faces and hairstyles are all unfamiliar to me. I know no one except Edward and the young woman who's served us.

Directly behind Edward is the partition of our booth and then the skinny hallway that leads several feet down, further out of sight to the restrooms. Anybody could've gone down the hall unnoticed.

"Did you see anybody head that way?" I ask.

Edward shakes his head.

"I went outside for a minute to make a call."

I can't tell if he believes me.

He glances around as if looking for something.

"I don't see any surveillance cameras. Maybe we should ask the staff."

"There's really no point." I hear the anxiety in my voice. All I want to do is get away from here, away from him. I need to get someplace alone so I may think clearly.

In a busy place like this just about anyone could go unnoticed. Now that Edward has paid the bill our waitress hasn't come by to check on us. We are customers who now must be on our way. She won't be any help. She remembers food orders, drink orders, big and small tippers, the special demands from wealthy people and celebrities who require more attention than the rest of us.

The people I saw minutes earlier seem like they've been replaced with new ones. Besides there's little chance the person who left the note made herself known. If anything, Becca probably covered her most obvious feature, that platinum hair, under a baseball cap.

Edward is on his feet like he's agitated or late for a meeting he's forgotten about. This lunch with me did not go as planned. All I've done is further complicate things, muddy up the investigation into his sister's disappearance with talk of a series of ominous notes that most likely have nothing to do with her. He must feel like he's wasted precious time.

I wonder if he too will use my former background working with the police against me and dismiss me as some kind of pathetic soul so bored with my current life figuring out the prices of condos, office buildings, the occasional precious parcel of unbuilt-on earth, a rare commodity in Southern California, that I'm willing to fabricate such disturbing notes and pretend like I'm rattled by them.

Years earlier when the police no longer needed my freelance assistance as often, I realized I never really liked my former job as a handwriting analyst to begin with. I didn't like reading into the strokes of every word. At times it betrayed the drastic lengths some people will go to hurt others.

Because of this skill, it's made me distrustful of practically everyone.

"Listen, Tia," Edward says, pointing to the folded paper towel with the note inside it in my hand.

His touch, when he takes my wrist and guides me up from the table, feels protective. In a fleeting moment I'm reminded he's Elise's older brother and I am her childhood friend.

"Whoever it might've been who left you that… well, you shouldn't leave here alone. Let me walk you to your car."

Traffic snakes so slowly on Laurel Canyon –
the steep fifteen miles long shortcut too many
commuters take instead of battling the bumper-
to-bumper freeway that is even worse. A relatively
minor hassle I've chosen to live with because in
return my peaceful two bedroom is far removed
from the city, the last home on the end of a curv-
ing asphalt road that turns into gravel. My closest
neighbor is a good two acres away, separated by
trees and brush and a mutual agreement that we
are grateful for the invaluable space of real estate
between us.

I brake to avoid a Tesla, with a back window
so dark it's probably illegal, that appears out of
nowhere to cut me off. Glen drives a similar
black model, though expensive cars like Tesla's
and Mercedes are everywhere in the LA area. Less
than ten miles from my place, it will be another
fifteen minutes before I reach it.

Outside the restaurant Edward suggested I give
him the note because he'd said he was heading to
the station to get an update from the detectives
on Elise's case.

It is a relief to have that note, *that word,* out of
my hands.

I did not have time to take a picture of the
note like I did the other two. I hadn't wanted to.
Considering the writer had used her left hand, I'd
gleaned as much from the note as I could anyway.
The main thing is to get Kyle out of my life for
good. The appraisal I promised I'd do for him in
Encino will be the last one I'll ever do for him.

I'm so angry at myself for allowing him to

manipulate me into prolonging the sale of the Marina Del Rey condo. That's probably what set off Becca.

In my rear view mirror a fire truck appears with its lights revolving and the siren blaring. I do my best to pull to the side of the road, turning the two front tires of my Prius. Most of the other drivers do the same except for the person behind the wheel of the Tesla. Another blast of the siren and then finally the driver heeds the call and makes just enough room for the fire truck to squeeze by.

It isn't until I turn the corner of my street and feel the smooth asphalt under my tires become unsteady gravel that I glimpse dark smoke unfurling into the sky. Either a neighbor's house is on fire or it's my own.

My mind is a jumble of possibilities, one more awful than the next. I hit the gas and take the next turn too sharply, nearly losing control of my car. I brake and straighten the wheel before hitting the metal mail box of a neighbor. I'm still five houses away from my own, nearly half of a mile.

The quiet shaded stretch and predictable curves of this road I typically slow down to enjoy is now taking too long to pass.

I feel like I won't ever reach the devastation that's waiting for me at the end of it.

This is what the note means.

Surprise!

I'll come home to be surprised to find *my beloved home* has burned to the ground.

I speed up, the sound of gravel kicking at the

sides of my car, nicking at the paint. Between the tall trees the smoke seems to be getting even darker.

I'm getting closer.

A neighbor must've spotted the smoke and called 911.

The fire truck is parked sideways, blocking entrance to my property. But it isn't my house with the roomy front porch where I host small dinner gatherings in the summertime with family and friends that is ablaze.

Several feet from the cement walk that leads to my front porch sits a BMW SUV, the same charcoal color as Elise's, the interior consumed by flames, fire swirling up out of the open sun roof. A gas accelerant must've been used, the kind that makes putting out the fire even more dangerous. The heat is an invisible wall that forces me back a few steps. My fear is felt in my throat at the thought.

Elise might be inside.

Two firemen stand on either side of the vehicle, one of them with water hose in hand, ready though only watching, because at this point there is little they can do but let it burn.

CHAPTER FIFTEEN

~Back Then~

*F*OR MEMORIAL WEEKEND *Jordan's par- ents invited Jordan and me to stay with them at their three-story beach house narrowly wedged between several others along Pacific Coast Highway in Santa Monica. I was only too excited to be included. I'd never met them before until then and being part of a family event was a sign our relationship was headed beyond the boundaries of the campus where Jordan and I went to school.*

While the two of us had just hit the three-month mark, my sister still had her concerns. Didn't I see how I acted around him? How easily he kept me quiet? She hadn't liked that when he'd come over to our home for dinner he'd dominated the conversation with stories about his many trips with his parents to Europe - countries like France, Norway and Spain. He was only nine when he'd stood inside the Parthenon in Greece. Laney thought he was a braggart, too self-confident and manipulative. My mother, a single parent of adult chil- dren, should test the waters, he'd told her. She'd listened. She was busy getting ready for her first solo trip as a widowed woman on a twelve-day cruise to the Carib- bean Islands with exotic stops at St. Maarten, Antigua and Tortola, among others.

Jordan's lawyer parents weren't as welcoming to me as my mother had been to Jordan that night she'd cooked him dinner, but they weren't especially warm to their son either. It was as if they were one step removed from him, like at any moment he would disappoint them and they had to be prepared. In fact, he should've graduated last semester, but he was having to retake two general education courses so he'd be able to come out with a B average and get into law school.

Inside the beach house, Jordan's parents took the master bedroom on the third floor which left Jordan and I with the two bedrooms on the second floor to choose from.

"You two should stay in the one with the better view of the water," Jordan's mother called out from the staircase which seemed strange considering her son was not a guest and clearly knew the layout of each room.

I was a little startled she was so open about Jordan and I sharing a room, something my mother, even though I was nearly nineteen, would never permit.

"Maybe I should unpack in the other room," I said, not wanting to be a tease.

"Hey, hey, hey, wait a minute."

Jordan caught me before I had a chance to get away and took me in his arms.

I inhaled his spicy scent of patchouli oil he wore instead of men's cologne.

He kissed me, then pulled back, his arms hooked loosely around my shoulders.

"It's okay, Tia," he said. "You're not ready to have sex with me yet. I get it. No big deal."

I felt myself tense up and start to pull away.

He only hung on to me tighter.

"That doesn't mean we can't sleep in the same bed. We'll just mess around, I promise."

For the next three days we browned on the sand stretched out on beach towels. If I laid on my stomach, Jordan took his time covering my shoulders, my back, then down my legs with suntan oil, sometimes slipping his hand playfully into my bikini bottoms. The waves weren't much, white caps that dissolved into froth, so instead of a surf board Jordan settled for a Boogie board to paddle belly down towards deeper water.

Jordan's parents retreated to their own separate parts of the house — his father dozing through pre-season baseball on the couch in the den while his mother chain-smoked and gabbed to a friend out on the third-floor balcony. At night his father cooked hamburgers or steaks on the barbecue and his mother ordered side dishes like three cheese macaroni salad and tomato cucumber salad with chickpeas and mint delivered from the gourmet grocery store a few blocks away.

Etiquette was a primary concern and Jordan's father made sure to always serve me first, then his wife. He seemed polite though relatively unconcerned about getting to know more about me than if I liked my meat cooked medium or well done.

I tried not to think about how many other girls Jordan had brought to this same beach house over the years. This time he'd brought me. He even introduced me to his parents as his steady girlfriend, letting them know we'd been going out for a few months. I wasn't just another one of his flings. At night, in bed together, he'd kiss me, his tongue moving in my mouth, his body rubbing up against mine, eventually coming to the touch of his hard cock against my hip.

"I love you, Tia," he said afterward. He'd curl up against me for a moment before stretching out on his back and falling asleep.

On the final morning I got up before Jordan and I was coming down the stairs towards the kitchen when I heard his parents in a heated conversation.

"How long do you expect this to last, Ronald?" Jordan's mother said, her husband's first name bitter on her lips.

"Honey."

"Don't you dare placate me. I'm not one of your adoring big-busted secretaries with her eyes wide and her legs spread even wider."

I held my breath, afraid to move, shift my weight and thereby announce my presence. Their marriage wasn't my business. I hadn't meant to eavesdrop. If they caught me standing there, it would ruin everything. They'd both hate me and Jordan wouldn't ask me on another family trip.

"Alright, alright." Jordan's father sighed. "Once he graduates at the end of the semester he'll lose interest."

"This one has lasted longer than the others."

"Yes."

"He's meant for so much more."

"I know and we'll help him achieve all of it. Once he gets his law degree, then he can think about settling down. It looks good for someone running for office to have a young family."

"This one might try and get herself pregnant."

"There's not much we can do about that."

"She's been good for him, a nice girl. But her father," Jordan's mother scoffs. "He sold tires. Black rubber for

Christ's sake. He might as well have been an insurance salesman or a greasy mechanic in coveralls."

The insult leveled at my father made my bare feet unsteady on the stairs. It knocked the wind right out of me. It made me want to flee from the beach house in nothing but the shorts and tank I had on. As a kid, when I had a bad case of strep throat, my father stayed up all night with me, spoon fed me ice chips he'd crushed from bulky cubes using a coffee mug and hummed Greek folk songs he'd learned from summers spent on the island of Syros with his yia yia and papous. He once drove me to two different counties and eight clothing stores in one day to find me the perfect dress for the sixth-grade dance. He was the kind of good father I could never stop missing and memory of a loving husband my mother could never outrun.

I was trapped with these heartless snobs from Hancock Park and I'd have to pretend for the next several hours that everything was fine until I was finally dropped off at my dorm. At the time I remember thinking my sister was right that dating Jordan would devastate me, only she was wrong he'd be the one to have done it.

CHAPTER SIXTEEN

NOBODY WILL LET me inside my own home. The police officers on hand are making me wait out here like some curious onlooker, like several of my neighbors who've made the trek over from their houses to see the charred remains of the SUV that burned to the ground practically in their own backyard. Yellow caution tape extends across the front porch of my home as well as cordoning off Elise's vehicle, forming a misshaped octagon. The tape sags in places then picks up in a slight gust of wind.

There is no need for an ambulance because thankfully there is no body in the SUV.

Elise could still be alive.

Whatever physical evidence that could link the person or persons behind her disappearance is lost to black ash.

I try Hugh's cell for the second time, but I'm sent directly to voice mail. I've already left one message. I don't see the reason for leaving another.

It's mid-afternoon and he should have his cell on him, in his back pocket where he always keeps it, even when he's on a site. Then I remember that long faint scratch that extended between his freckled shoulder blades.

I see Hugh's cell phone turned off on the nightstand. I see thin white linen sheets, tangled up from lovemaking, I see the raised point of a woman's nipple, I see my fiancé bending over the woman's chest to kiss it. I see a soft sea breeze coming in through the open window, cooling off two naked bodies, a couple having sex for pleasure not pregnancy.

The owner of the elaborate three level beach house Hugh is working on is a divorcee', a studio executive's ex who's taken him to the cleaners with no prenup. She could be a real knockout for all I know. I've never seen her.

Hugh has spoken about this woman like he would any client, just another job, a bank account with unlimited resources that will allow for top-of-the-line building materials while also adding another high digit to his 401K, helping him get that much closer to retirement.

But creating disinterest about the person one's secretly bedding is common when someone is having an affair. He could've gotten pointers from his sleazy friend Glen on how best to pull off being unfaithful. For all I know maybe Hugh cheated on his first wife, the one who tragically drowned.

I turn off my cell as Detective Ramirez and his female partner get out of his sedan. She's a thick woman with short blonde hair, a pantsuit and gold aviator shades. He introduces her but I don't pay attention to her name. All I want is inside my own house.

A news van has arrived and a man in a suit is setting up to give his report from my front yard. This is leading news for the upcoming five o'clock hour – what appears to be key evidence in Elise Davis's missing persons' case, her vehicle, that she was believed to be driven away in on the day of her disappearance, now a steel skeleton, hollowed out by heat and flames.

I look away, afraid the reporter will somehow figure out who I am and his cameraman will film me.

Detective Ramirez is slowly circling the wreckage, his arms folded at his chest. Clearly, he appears a little blown away by the fact that the outside of my residence is now part of his crime scene.

"We'll need to head down to the station and get your statement," his female partner says to me.

"Can't we do it inside?" I ask.

All I can think about is getting into my house, shutting out the sight of Elise's vehicle, the police and TV crews. There is the cold unsettling knowledge that the person who's left me the notes is directly connected to Elise's abduction.

Bringing the evidence to my doorstep, then lighting it on fire is not only bold, it's a form of bragging. The police must be so far off with their investigation he or she isn't remotely worried about being caught. At this point Elise could very well be dead.

Detective Ramirez shakes his head as he approaches his partner and me.

"Forensics hasn't gotten here yet. The investigation is going to take some time. Best if we stay out of their way."

I nod, but I know he's lying. The truth is he wants to get me to an interview room so I may be videotaped. Definitively it's Elise's vehicle that has been abandoned mere feet from the front of my house. Although blackened, all the numbers and letters on the front license plate are still visible. It's obvious by Detective Ramirez's presence the plates are a match with Elise's gray BMW SUV.

I don't want to have to do this alone. We'll go to the police station. It won't be the one downtown, the one I'm familiar with, where I once worked. So much time has passed since I was brought in on a case to analyze, all the detectives and officers who had truly believed in me, who believed in the study behind what I used to do are mostly retired, transferred somewhere else or got out of law enforcement altogether.

My police force allies are slim to none.

I really am on my own.

Is there anyone I can call besides Hugh? My sister Laney is another state away. My mother is a clear continent or two from here. Jessica is most likely at work. By the time she's able to break away from her clients and make it across town the ordeal at the station will be over. Kyle is certainly not an option, especially when his new girlfriend could be the one who left this burned out wreckage for me to deal with.

Surprise!

The one word on the Post-it note that was left

on the mirror for me in the women's restroom only a couple hours before is chilling to me now. Kyle keeps reminding me how much I don't know about my fiancé, but how much does he really know about the woman who's entwined herself so effortlessly into his life? Had Becca written threatening notes to her former lover and that's why a restraining order had been filed against her? Was she capable of harming a woman whom she didn't even know just to get back at me, the person whom to her is a romantic rival?

"Ms. Wilkins." Detective Ramirez calls me by my married name. "We should probably take my car."

I hate the way Kyle's last name sounds off the detective's tongue like I'm the odd person out of a love triangle. I hate that I haven't legally changed back to my maiden name, something I should've done several months ago as soon as I finalized the divorce papers.

I look at my Prius that is now boxed in behind another news van and two squad cars. There is no way out of here unless I get a ride from someone else.

Inside the backseat of the detective's sedan, with Ramirez and his female partner in front, I know what I look like as the car passes the growing crowd of onlookers, news reporters and the cameras filming our departure. I look guilty.

CHAPTER SEVENTEEN

DETECTIVE RAMIREZ'S PHYSICALLY intimidating female partner shows me to a plain cramped room with a black table and three plastic chairs. I'm not offered a bottle of water or anything else to drink. I'm not even asked one single question by this woman. She stares down at a file in her hand, checks something on the screen of her phone, never making eye contact with me. The way she's ignoring me makes me uncomfortable which might be the point. I'll be relieved when her partner shows up and want to immediately start talking.

I'm fully aware of this strategy. I've seen it before with the investigators I used to work with. If I were able to track down someone I knew who was still on the force and ask for their help, explain how I've found myself on the wrong side of the table in an interrogation room, I realize it would be too late. The physical evidence is compelling. A missing woman's car was found burning in front of my home. There is no way out of answering Ramirez and his partner's questions unless I lawyer up. Even if that's the smartest thing to do, I am innocent and I'll find my own way out of this by telling the truth.

"I'm sorry for keeping you, Catia."

Detective Ramirez appears with a ceramic cup of steaming coffee he sets in front of me. He's shed his sports coat and the sleeves of his business shirt are rolled up to the elbows.

"Safe to drink, I swear. No stale coffee left on all day in a coffeemaker for us. We have a couple of Keurig machines. It's fresh. Decaf. Do you take it black?"

I nod.

I wouldn't mind adding creamer, but I don't plan on sticking around long enough to take more than a couple sips. Yet again, I glance down at my phone, wishing Hugh would call me back. The wallpaper on my phone is a photograph of my father and me standing in front of the gaping backdrop of the Grand Canyon, the summer before he died. It's one of the many old family pictures Laney had transferred onto computer and sent to me, knowing it was particularly special. Every year we planned a vacation to a national park. I'm wearing a sun visor, shorts and a t-shirt with a colorful rainbow on it. My father is forever young, handsome and proud he's standing in front of one of nature's greatest treasures, his arm around one of his two daughters. Although his dark features were not a match with my green eyes and light brown hair, there was no denying by our expressions he and I were family. He was so happy to be with both of his girls. Laney had been on the other side of the little black Kodak camera lens, taking the picture. Our mother was in line getting us tickets for the mule ride that trailed down to the bottom. No matter how old I get I don't ever want to forget the look I had on my face that day. It was when I still felt completely safe, my father's hand firmly on my shoulder, and I was unaware of what I would encounter later in life, the cruel and ugly things people can do to each other when they think love is over.

Detective Ramirez settles in the chair next to his partner, looking comfortable.

I get the feeling he is about to strike.

"Why do you think someone would park Ms. Davis's SUV out front of your home and torch it?" he asks.

"I don't know."

"Other than yourself and your boyfriend, who else knew you wouldn't be home at that time today?"

I shrug. It bothers me the detective doesn't refer to Hugh as my fiancé, though I stop myself from correcting him.

"I'm an appraiser, so I'm gone a lot during the day. Someone could've taken a gamble and assumed I wouldn't be home for a while. It'd be a safe bet."

"Only you weren't working today. You were with Elise's brother?"

"Edward. He wanted to talk with me about the day she went missing. He said he was coming by here after we'd had lunch."

"Yes, he was here."

Before I have a chance to ask about whether

Edward handed over the Post-It note, the female detective slides the file over to Ramirez and he opens it and pulls out three clear evidence bags, all three notes that have been left for me.

He lifts each bag one at a time, reading the note inside aloud, as if trying to make sense out of it, before tossing the bag back on the table. I don't need to hear the notes being read to me. I can picture them in my head. The first one is a statement, the other is a question and the last note is a one-word exclamation.

He is here early.

ARE YOU HOPEFUL SHE IS STILL ALIVE?

Surprise!

When put together the underlying messages are clear. I am watching you. I am curious if you know who I am. I am frustrated you aren't doing more to stop me. I know what the writer is doing, but obviously the detective doesn't get it if he still suspects I might be responsible for writing them.

"Someone's certainly trying to get your attention," he says. "We checked them for prints, but all we found are yours on the first two and none on the third one."

The room is getting colder, a shot of arctic air blasting down from the ceiling vent. I take a drink of the coffee. It is good, not a generic grocery store brand. I feel the coffee warming me, making the conditions tolerable, and I wonder if this is another manipulative tactic by the detective at getting me to talk.

"I told you after I *handed* you both the first and the second note," I add, letting him know I know the investigation he's conducting is sloppy and he's made at least one big mistake, leaving his prints on the first two notes. "I thought they might be connected to Elise."

He ignores my comment just as he doesn't bother asking for my professional assessment, a handwriting profile, of all three notes, how they are written and who might be behind them. For instance, I could share with him how the person behind the notes knows my background and is using every tactic to throw me off from using capital letters to writing in the crease to strain the shape of the words. The last note, written using the writer's untrained hand in such jagged lettering in red ballpoint, is a warning that things are escalating. It makes sense the writer resorted to doing something violent after writing it like setting fire to Elise's vehicle.

"And, according to Mr. Davis he said you apparently found this last note," the female partner speaks up. "In the ladies' room, on the mirror."

Her tone is incredulous and I'm suddenly angry at myself for agreeing to come down here to be interviewed in the first place. I should've been stubborn and insisted I be let inside my own home where I could've asked them to leave.

This is no longer an interview. It is an interrogation.

I glance down at my phone in my lap. Still no message from Hugh. *Where the hell is he?*

Detective Ramirez slightly smiles at me when I look up, sensing they've pushed me too far and I'm about to get up out of this chair and walk out. Clearly, by the special treatment I'm being given, they haven't gotten very far with their investigation. I may be their only lead. He tells his partner he can handle the rest of the interview on his own and he waits until she leaves before he continues questioning me.

"Who do you think could be behind this, Catia? You told me yourself the other day you and Ms. Davis hadn't been in contact for some time except for the day she disappeared."

"My husband," I begin, stumbling, aware of how self-conscious I sound. "I mean, my ex-husband, Kyle, has a new girlfriend. Her name is Rebecca, Rebecca Dennison."

The detective listens carefully yet doesn't write down her name which frustrates me.

"What is her connection to you other than she is dating your ex-husband?"

I rest my elbows on the table in an attempt to stay calm otherwise the detective might doubt what I'm telling him.

"Nothing, it's just. She has a restraining order against her from a past relationship. And she's…"

"How do you know this?" the detective cuts in.

"Kyle told me."

"Does she have some reason to be jealous of you?" Detective Ramirez leans closer as if it's just the two of us and there isn't a camera in the high corner of the room filming our every move. "Are you romantically involved with your ex-husband?"

I push back some in my seat, accidentally knocking the table and some coffee splashes out of my cup.

"Of course not. Hugh is not my boyfriend. He's my fiancé. He lives at my house during part of the week. Whoever left Elise's car was taking a big risk."

Detective Ramirez pulls out a Kleenex from a box on the table and wipes up the coffee. Some witnesses and even potential murderers must cry in this room reliving the grisly images they've walked in on or the bloody act they thought they'd gotten away with committing.

That worn tattoo on the inside of the detective's wrist is visible and I wonder if he got it a long time ago while working undercover as a gang member. He could be an expert at playing along with any situation, never showing his hand, which makes him the kind of detective that will inevitably solve Elise's case even if it means finding only her remains.

"What is your fiancé's last name?"

"Roberts."

Detective Ramirez writes something down. By the movements of his hand I can tell it's the letters in Hugh's last name. How did my fiancé suddenly seem more like a person worth looking into further than Kyle's crazed girlfriend with the restraining order against her? Was it because of his outburst at the house after hearing about the notes? Hugh had been concerned about my safety. He has no reason to want to harm me.

"Any fiancé would've reacted the way Hugh did the other day when he overheard us talking about the notes. He's protective."

The detective's expression makes it seem like he's curious why I'm still talking about Hugh when in his mind he's already moved on.

"Think for just a second," he tells me. "Do you and Elise have any shared enemies?"

Hours before, Elise's handsome brother chased me into the women's restroom of the restaurant using only his words. His line about me being at the heart of every tragedy his family has ever experienced felt as unexpected as piano wire snaked around my neck, squeezing off my airways. Had that been his intention?

To get me up from the table and into the women's restroom so either he or someone else could plant the note? What makes me think he couldn't be a part of this? Some sweet grown-up kiss when I was twelve that his sister had actually put him up to?

It makes no sense, if he holds me responsible for his mother's death, why he'd wait all these years later to come after me and his sister. Revenge, I remind myself, may not always make sense to the target, but it definitely does to the one exacting it. Maybe it has more to do with his father's lingering illness, the way it has been carefully covered up by the family. How much will Edward inherit if his sister is dead? Does he know Deborah is pregnant? If he has done something to his sister, are Deborah and the baby in danger?

I wouldn't be here being interviewed by the police if I hadn't agreed to meet him for lunch. Most likely I would've stayed home and the person who'd taken Elise wouldn't dared to have risked being seen by me.

The truth is I don't think my interview so far has done much to rule me out as a suspect. The possibility remains I'm somehow doing this all for attention, the notes, even apparently, Elise's burned out car.

My mind goes all sorts of ways. By boldly planting the evidence in my own front yard, I could be attempting to turn attention in another direction. Or maybe Edward is already setting a trap for me. Maybe Edward is making things up to the detective like I've always been envious of Elise's wealth or he could know about the baby her wife is growing inside her and use that against me.

Money buys knowledge, no matter how private, and he could've found out how badly I want a baby. I divorced my husband because he wanted to keep me childless. Edward could've said something more when he came into the station earlier with the last note, how he thinks I'm emotionally troubled, how he didn't see anyone else enter the ladies restroom except me.

Elise, I realize, could already be dead. The fire is a means of doing away with any possible DNA evidence.

The police are wasting precious time on me, plain and simple. Pointing this out, however, is useless. I'll have to use my own methods to find out what's happened to her.

"Catia," the detective says my name. "Do you have a shared enemy with Ms. Davis?"

"No," I lie to the detective. "There's no one."

Hugh is waiting for me by his truck in the parking lot outside the station after I'm done being interviewed. Something is wrong like he's feeling guilty or he's known by not being here when I called him, this is the first time he's let me down.

He pulls me into a powerful hug, then gently kisses my forehead.

"I'm so sorry I wasn't here for you."

For a moment I give in to the strength of his embrace, how it steadies me. I'm aware of how physically weak I now feel.

"It's okay," I say, although if he had been here for the last thirty-five minutes while I was being interviewed by the police he could've sat in with me or at least I could've known he was right outside the door. Instead I kept picturing him having sex with another woman. Part of me is ashamed for thinking the worst of him.

"No, it isn't." Hugh pulls away from me. "I should've told you the truth a while ago."

Something drops inside me and I'm not sure if I'm still standing. Two male police officers pass by us with sodas and bags of fast food in their hands. One is laughing at something the other says. They're both young, probably both single. I hate how happy they are just as my fiancé is about to tell me something that will crush me.

"What is it, Hugh?"

He runs a hand through his hair. Finally, I notice he's in a clean black t-shirt and black jeans. He hasn't been at a construction site at all today. I have a sick understanding that I'm right about him having an affair with the studio exec's ex-wife. He doesn't want to marry me anymore. I'm too young and want too much. He's thought about it and doesn't want to start another family with me, not at his age.

"I missed your calls because I had my phone turned off. I was at the doctor's office."

A part of me panics. The sudden shift in concern from infidelity to his health makes it hard for me to think straight.

"The doctor's? Why? Are you sick?"

Hugh takes a deep breath.

"No. Nothing like that."

"Then what is it?"

"Shortly after we met, once I realized I was falling in love with you, I had a procedure done to reverse the vasectomy I'd had while married to Carolyn. She'd had a difficult pregnancy with Ashley. She didn't want any more kids."

He's still explaining himself to me, rushing to get the words out, it's all been weighing on him, he meant to tell me sooner, something about a test, the odds of him having viable sperm.

Through the noise he's making, I'm only able to focus on one thing.

"How long ago did you have it done?" My voice doesn't sound like my own. I see how Hugh is startled by it

"About seven weeks ago," he says.

CHAPTER EIGHTEEN

~Back Then~

JORDAN TOLD ME not to give what his parents said about me or my family a second thought. I finally let him know several weeks later that I'd overheard them talking at the beach house because he'd wanted me to go to their house in Hancock Park for dinner, and I kept coming up with excuses. "They're fucking snobs," he insisted. "I hate what they said about your old man."

I flinched at the words "old man." My father died at thirty-seven. He was hardly an old man.

A part of me wanted Jordan to go back to his fraternity house and his so-called brothers, but there was no chance of that happening. My mother was off on another trip, this time a ten day stay on Maui.

Jordan and my friends wanted to throw a party at my mother's new house in Los Alamitos, a city famous for a racetrack and little else. It's the place where my mother decided on relocating to shortly after I decided to apply to Long Beach State, so she could be closer to me. Some of my friends and Kyle's would hitch rides off campus for the ten- mile drive, but turnout wouldn't nearly be as high if it were actually in Long Beach, within walking distance back to the university.

Three more weeks before Jordan graduated. He'd been trying to convince me to join him all summer back-packing across Europe, staying in hostels in Sweden, Amsterdam, France, even taking a boat out to Greece, maybe looking up a couple of my distant relatives, the ones I'd only heard about but had never met. "Who knows," Jordan joked. "Maybe we'll come back married. My parents would just have to suck it up and get used to calling you my wife."

He meant well with the half-hearted proposal and I appreciated the thoughtfulness about going to Greece, I did.

But after spending a year in the dorms sharing such a small room with another girl I was craving my own space, my privacy, four walls and the kind of silence that wasn't suddenly interrupted by other girls barging in asking to bum a couple bucks off me or badgering me to tag along with them to the cafeteria for dinner.

Besides I was hoping to get used to life without Jordan in it. Our relationship, whether he wanted to admit it or not, was over.

The right strings were pulled and even with Jordan's spotty grades, he was going to start USC Law School in the fall. Although he often disagreed with them, in the end, he'd do what his parents wanted him to do.

I'd rather end it before he and I argued over it and came to that conclusion together.

Jordan sensed I was pulling away from him which made him hang around me all the more.

We were at Costco with a shopping cart, loading up on cheap booze for the party. Jim Beam. Popov. A few cases of Natural Light.

Jordan smiled at me from down the aisle and I

thought I smiled back. Instead of being pumped-up for a night of partying with our friends, I was actually, quietly to myself, dreading it.

CHAPTER NINETEEN

AFTER EVERYTHING THAT'S happened today with Elise's car being set on fire in front of my house, a grim calling card by her abductor, Hugh refuses to leave me alone and insists on sleeping on the couch.

I don't put up much of a fight because I'm exhausted by his confession in the parking lot of the police station.

He hasn't cheated on me with another woman. He's cheated me out of time, weeks upon weeks I'd been counting on that together we've been trying for a baby.

I even began to suspect it was me that my eggs are bad or I have an undiagnosed medical issue with my uterus, because each month when I took the pregnancy test kit in the bathroom the stick came back negative.

What he's done, what he's lied to me about is another form of betrayal, one that hurts more than if he's bedded that studio exec's ex-wife. I'd prepared myself for adultery yet I've been blind-sided by the fact he's sterile.

If he's telling me the truth and he's had the procedure done to reverse his vasectomy seven weeks ago, I've lost at least twelve weeks, counting the time before he actually scheduled the surgery and then went through with it. He claims he has the proof, if I'll just come in with him and let the doctor explain it to me, that his sperm are alive and undamaged by the reversal.

I've told him I can't right now, not with Elise's abductor out there making me play a part in her disappearance as if I should somehow know the reason why. A part of me prefers Hugh in the house, just not in my bed.

He agrees to follow me home and stay downstairs. He understands why I can't look at him.

A couple media vans are still staked out just beyond my gravel driveway. Minutes before eleven tonight the reporters inside will appear alert and perfectly dressed. They'll stand in front of their cameraman, all lit up, prepared to give their final report of the night live in front of a darkened house, *my house*.

With the remnants of Elise's SUV hauled away, earlier footage will be shown, the dramatic flames the firemen couldn't immediately put out because a gas accelerant must've been used, then my face in the backseat of Detective Ramirez's sedan as I'm driven to the station to be questioned.

I lay in the dark, in my bed and although I can't sleep, I also can't close my eyes. When I do I keep picturing Elise's body abandoned like trash several yards deep along a roadside the volunteer searchers haven't thought to look. Her killer doesn't bother burying her because part of the plan is that the body *is* found.

Elise's face is turned to one side and it's pale and purpled because she's been strangled. Her blue eyes are wide open in fear, caught in that terrifying moment right before death, and I see the mud or is it blood dried under her French tip manicured fingernails because the Elise I grew up with would claw and scratch and put up one hell of a fight to save her own life.

I'm awakened by the sound of someone knocking on my front door. I roll over. The clock on my nightstand reads fifteen after nine. Hugh must've gone to work because the knocking continues, a little louder this time, with more force added.

The person at the door knows I'm home.

I pull on jeans, fasten a bra, cover up with a clean black t-shirt. As I head down the stairs, my whole body aches, the fatigue from lack of sleep. The shell-shocked feeling resurfaces, the knowledge my fiancé has lied to me in the cruelest possible way.

A co-conspirator with my barren womb.

I must've finally dozed off somewhere after five, right before dawn. It's going to be a long day, one I instantly regret because of what I know I have to do – track down the person behind Elise's disappearance.

Through the peephole I see a man in a workman's uniform, a tool box in his hand. Axel's Locksmith Company stitched on a patch on his shirt.

"I'm here to change all the locks on your doors, ma'am," he calls out.

"Just a minute," I say. In the kitchen I grab my cell out of my purse and see Hugh's text.

For safe measure, he's made arrangements for my locks to be changed. He hopes I understand and he hasn't overstepped his bounds. It's just like Hugh not to allow our argument yesterday to distract him from his plan of protecting me while he's not here.

Under any other circumstances, I'd return his text and thank him, but doing that might make Hugh think things are good again between us when they aren't.

I go back out to the foyer and open the door. While the workman is changing out the back-door's lock, I make a fresh pot of coffee, then boot up my computer. A photo of Elise's charred SUV is the first news story to appear. I shiver inside upon recognizing the white steps leading up to my front porch, my front window with the gauzy drapes that allow in the sunlight. It suddenly occurs to me that those drapes must illuminate me from inside my home when I turn on the lights should someone be watching me from the outside at night.

If I check my email, I'm positive I'll come across a dozen or more TV reporters and journal-ists from reputable papers and blog sites who've tracked me down, all wanting me to give them an interview, ask me hard questions I don't have the answers to. By now they've probably dug up our childhood in the form of elementary school photos – incomplete smiles with a stump of an adult tooth growing in or a baby one just lost, long stringy hair, a freshly brushed pony tail. Feverishly, in order to be the first one with the story, the swarm of media will try and piece it together – the connection between Elise and I must mean something. It definitely means something to the person who took Elise. I, myself, don't know what it is for sure.

I have no plans of looking at my email and find myself on UCLA's faculty webpage. In the search frame, Kyle's faculty number immediately pops up as I guessed it would from all the times he used my computer out of convenience here at home instead of his own. Before he left he should've thought of erasing all traces of himself, including my computer. He knows I'm not the type to buy the newest piece of technology and replace something only when it stops working.

I type in his password, the one he uses for just about everything – the last name of his favorite baseball player, retired New York Yankees first baseman, Don Mattingly and the number forty-six, along with an exclamation point. The password unlocks the kind of crucial information I need – student records.

The site is confidential and I know I'm breaking all kinds of privacy laws. Normally this would stop me, and I'd try some other way. But yesterday someone made this very personal. Not someone. . . Becca. She made all of this about me. The note left in the women's restroom, Elise's SUV burning up on my property, the cops seriously contemplating whether I've had something to do with her disappearance, all of it has been done to get my attention, to get me to act.

I'm prepared to deal with the consequences if I get caught. At least I'll get a handle on Becca's past. I can't be wrong, not about this.

Academic records can be as revealing as a criminal one, which Becca doesn't have. I checked the day before on that using a credit card and a sketchy online site.

Soon I'm looking at her GPA, a lukewarm 3.2. She's barely making graduate level grades which is a 3.0.

I scroll down past the semester grades from Spring of this year when she first came to Southern California. I'm surprised to find she's an Educational Administration major. Becca, with her emotional instability and protective order against her, wants to work with kids. I just assumed she met Kyle in one of his history classes. She took one semester off before transferring from the University of New Mexico. She only stayed at that school for one semester and earned an A in one class and then received an Unofficial Withdrawal in the other.

The prestigious schools she's attended suggest she's highly intelligent. I could go as far back as the bachelor's degree from an Ivy League school, Brown University, when her major was different, though I'm more concerned about the last couple years. Like I assumed, there's a sizeable gap between her graduating from Brown and enrolling at UNM.

Quickly, I do the Math – she's thirty-one. She's lying to Kyle about her age, which is not exactly a crime. Many women do it.

It's not the professor who gave her the high grade at UNM I'm interested in talking to – it's the one who signed the form allowing her to leave the class well after she'd passed the deadline to drop it. There is no name next to the grade, this isn't a high school report card, so I'll have to do my own digging.

The landline rings. When I reach the phone in the family room I see it's my sister Laney and decide not to pick up. Did footage of my house, of me, make it all the way to Oregon? Laney isn't big on the Internet and spends most of her days homeschooling her three small children. She'd have to catch it during the early morning news on TV.

I assumed Elise's SUV being found just made the local news yesterday and national media outlets are more preoccupied with Carson Davis's death - anticipation over when his funeral will take place, a real celebrity free-for-all. He is Hollywood royalty, Elise is merely biological offspring. Her life, even her death, is only as important as how closely the outcome ties in with her famous father.

The locksmith has broken out the drill for the back door, the noise so earsplitting I move my laptop and cup of coffee into the family room. What I'm about to do is most likely going to get me into trouble and it's important that I think straight. Thankfully, when I part the drapes I don't see any news trucks, only my car and the locksmith's white van.

Once online again, I punch in the faculty listing for the Education department at UNM. The class Becca received the unofficial withdrawal in is specifically taught by a male professor – youngish, maybe my age, mid-thirties. He doesn't look her type. His face is chubby and Midwestern red, a wholesome nerd.

His office number is next to his photo and title. Before I lose my nerve, I dial. I'm not exactly sure what I'm going to say. Should it go directly to voice mail, I can't leave my name or number. I'll just have to hang up and try again later.

In three rings he actually picks up.

"Dr. Barrett."

His voice is smug, no "hello" from him. He wants to remind everyone of his "doctor" status.

I think fast and tell him I'm from the Los Angeles County Superintendent's office and Miss Rebecca Dennison has applied for a position. I leave out my name, keeping things vague, because I figure this guy is so concerned with people taking up his precious time he'll want to get me off the phone as soon as he can anyway.

Dr. Barrett says nothing. A couple seconds pass. I'm afraid he's about to hang up on me.

"I really don't understand why she'd give my name as a personal reference. I don't know her."

I take a moment like I'm checking something. Recently I'm getting better at pretending.

"That's what it says here, Dr. Barrett."

"I can't speak for her academic capabilities as she did not complete my class. What's this position for?"

Damn. Come up with something, anything.

"Interning for a principal of an elementary school." Before he has a chance to challenge me any further on the details, I keep talking. "As you know, working with children requires a lot of patience. This position requires hands-on time with kids in the classroom as well as helping with administrative duties."

The professor doesn't comment, but it seems by his silence he might agree with me.

"What I can do is give you the name of my graduate assistant teacher. Her name's Meghan." He rattles off the number so fast I am hardly able to jot it down. "She was in that same class with Miss Dennison and might be able to better answer your question about her temperament."

The line goes dead.

So I am getting somewhere. Already, I know there's more to why Becca left that school after only one semester. I had asked about Becca's *patience.* Dr. Barrett's the one who changed it to *temperament.*

I hold off on calling the graduate assistant teacher until the locksmith is finished changing the lock to the front door and leaves me the shiny new key. Even though I'm still so angry with Hugh, I'm grateful to him for reassuring me I *am* safer in my home now than I was a day before.

The graduate student answers on the first ring. She's out of breath as if moving from one place to another. I hear traffic on her end like she's in the city.

Her breath changes after I mention Becca's name. The girl on the other end must be standing completely still.

"Dr. Barrett gave you my number?" She sounds suspicious, more street smart than her professor.

"Yes," I say, worried she's about to clam up. "He said you got to know her when the two of you were in his class a couple years ago."

"I'm probably not the best person to ask about her."

"That makes you the perfect person to ask. Please," I urge the girl. "I need you to tell me what you know about her."

At this point I've likely blown what little cover I have left. If Becca and Meghan are friends, Meghan can easily give my number that's shown up on her phone screen to Becca and I'm caught.

Between using my ex-husband's password in order to retrieve confidential records and impersonating a potential employer, I'll be the one with a restraining order against her for harassment.

I take a deep breath, willing her to tell me everything.

"Rebecca was dating a friend of mine," Meghan begins, talking fast to get this unpleasant conversation over with. "They weren't exclusive. It was casual. My friend told her she wasn't looking for anything serious. Rebecca claimed she understood. Then one morning after this other girl came out of my friend's place, Rebecca walked right up to her and beat her up bad with a tire iron. She must've been waiting out in the parking lot all night. The girl's eye socket was shattered.

Her front tooth was knocked out. Her jaw was broken. My friend got a restraining order against her. Rebecca was kicked out of school. Not exactly kicked out, more like she was asked to leave and never come back."

"Did the girl file charges on Rebecca?" I ask, remembering to use Becca's formal first name. This whole grisly scene explains why Becca only goes by her nickname now.

"No," Meghan says. "She was too scared. Shortly after she was released from the hospital she left school too. Went back home to heal up."

Meghan's voice is momentarily blipped by the sound of call waiting which I ignore.

"Do you know what Rebecca told her after she ruined her face?"

I don't answer because I can't imagine how this story could get any worse. I'm picturing the blood pulsing over her pretty features, a girl who lay stunned and helpless on the ground, struggling to cry out with a loose, dislocated jaw.

How could Kyle invite a woman like this into his life? Into his bed? How could he not know what she's capable of?

"She stood over her and said, 'I guess you won't be kissing another woman's bitch anymore now, will you?'"

My call waiting goes off again and this time I panic when I look down at the number flashing, demanding I respond, because it isn't Laney calling.

It's my ex-husband.

CHAPTER TWENTY

I DON'T KNOW HOW Kyle has found out so quickly about my using his password to access Becca's transcripts. Maybe he gets some kind of alert via text or email if it's from a foreign computer or IP address, one he doesn't use frequently. He hasn't used mine in well over a year, though he'll recognize it as soon as he sees it.

How can he be involved with a woman sick enough to shatter someone's eye socket with a tire iron? Sure, he'd sounded enamored by Becca's explosive temper that he'd mistakenly took as passion after finding out about the restraining order filed against her by her former lover, but there's no way he knows the extent of it, the fact she hospitalized a romantic rival.

Becca could've killed her.

My cell goes off. It's Kyle again.

The last time he couldn't get a hold of me he stopped by my house and waited on my front porch for me, so I get my keys and purse and I leave. I know my ex-husband and I know he'll want answers why I've used his password and hacked into the school's computer for his new girlfriend's records. He won't be understanding like Hugh would, hearing me out with an open mind. He'll be furious.

Although I've driven the road I live on innumerable times, I have trouble with the curves and hear the tires peel. I don't like what's happening to me. I'm being reckless, making stupid mistakes like using my own cell to call the people at UNM. If I'd thought about it first, I could've easily bought a burner phone so there would be no way to trace the calls back to me.

Once the stop sign comes into view, I let up on the gas and coast until I reach busy Laurel Canyon Boulevard. As I make a left-hand turn, I spot the police cruiser parked off on the side of the road.

Should I feel protected or alarmed?

If Detective Ramirez wants me followed, he wouldn't call for an obvious black and white patrol car, he'd request a bland colored sedan and the likelihood of me even spotting it tailing me would be slim.

Seeing this squad car is coincidence.

Kyle could be on his way over now and I hope I don't pass him. I'm taking a chance, heading in the same direction of the campus where he teaches, only I'll be turning soon and driving to the other side of town, where Jessica has her own small interior design firm. If confronted by my ex-husband, he'll accuse me of checking up on Becca because I'm overrun with jealousy. It will only be about him, the fact he's sharing his bed with her and I, as the ex-wife, simply can't take it. I must sabotage their relationship. Like the detective, he too will have trouble seeing a possible connection between Becca, the notes and Elise's disappearance. He's a professor and he's used to talking over others, and if provoked, he won't let me get a word in much less tell him about his girlfriend's violent past.

———◆———

Kyle and I first met on a packed plane from La Guardia airport bound for LAX. We'd both been given aisle seats parallel with each other. I'd spent a few days with my mother in London before she headed off on a tour of Ireland and Scotland. Kyle had been in New York City where he applied for a tenure-track job at Columbia University.

Whenever someone asked, we'd joke it was a forced first date – one we couldn't escape from because we were thirty thousand feet up in the air.

For the next four hours we got to know each other, watched a movie, shared a meal – a snack bag of cool ranch Doritos and split a wrapped hoagie he'd bought earlier inside the airport that had an expiration date on it.

Everything about Kyle threw me off in a good way. I fell for his bright blue eyes in contrast with his black hair and how he seemed cocky one minute and self-deprecating the next. He said he thought he'd aced the Columbia interview until right at the end when he got something caught in his throat and experienced a brief coughing fit.

He threw his arms up as high as he could and

not elbow the lady in the center seat next to him. "Why why why didn't I bring a bottle of water with me?"

"Why didn't the ones interviewing you offer you a glass of water when you first sat down?" I point out.

I could tell by the way he looked at me he liked I was taking his side. With his short haircut and wrinkled button down he looked like a high school intern, not a guy old enough to have the necessary degrees to be a professor.

"You know, I don't know. That's a good question. How impolite of them. They really should have. Next time I'm acing it and hiding a cough drop in the far back of my cheek."

I told him how dirty the Thames River was, keeping the conversation on my side surface level, about my trip, because I hadn't gone out with anybody since Jordan and I was unwilling to talk personally with anyone yet. After Kyle point blank asked whether there was a guy who'd be picking me up at the airport and I didn't answer, he caught on and seemed fine not to press me further.

Before we landed he took his chances and asked me out on a date and we agreed on a place and time to meet, dusk at the Griffith Park Observatory to look up at the stars. He'd grinned and said he'd already taken me to dinner and a movie so we'd already been there and done that. He was so confident I'd show up he didn't ask me for my number.

"What the *fuck* is going on?"

I'm greeted by Jessica's frankness as I enter her office, a stylish walk-up in Westwood, mostly comprised of glass and touches of mahogany and vanilla white furniture. She's ditched her heels under her desk and gone barefoot. She is the boss of her own business.

"Last night I see my closest friend being driven off in the backseat of a police car like she's starring in an episode of *Dateline*."

It's a few minutes past one. Jessica's secretary must still be at lunch.

I'm relieved to see her. So much has happened since we picked out my wedding dress only a few days ago at Gia's boutique. The happiness I experienced that day feels removed from me like it belongs to somebody else.

"The police needed to question me."

I leave out Detective Ramirez subtly inquiring about my lunch with Elise's brother, reinforcing my own alibi.

"I'm not...my car was blocked by the fire trucks and..."

"Jesus Christ, Tia." Jessica's voice is low, underscoring her concern. "Why would someone leave her car *at your place*."

"I don't know."

"Hugh must be freaking out. I'm surprised he's not attached at your hip right now, claw hammer in hand." As an interior designer Jessica knows the tools of a construction worker's trade since she occasionally consults with them on a job.

I wish she hadn't brought up Hugh because

he's a reminder of what *I'm missing*. It's selfish of me to think this way when Elise could still be alive, locked in a room somewhere desperate at the thought she'll never be able to come home and be present for the birth of her own child. I feel like I'm about to cry for her or maybe for me.

"What is it?" Jessica asks.

I confide in her about what Hugh confessed to me in the parking lot of the police station – the vasectomy he had while being married to Carolyn, how he started seriously dating me knowing how much I wanted a baby and he had no sperm. During those early months when we first had sex, he acted as if he *could get me pregnant*. I'd never had any reason to doubt him.

She listens carefully, weighing it all, not interrupting or passing judgment.

"Tia," she finally says. "You are in a good relationship. Hugh loves you. I think those procedures are fairly simple to reverse. But even if they aren't – worst case scenario the two of you can adopt."

I nod, expecting her to take my side. Instead her words leave me cold.

The word "adopt" feels clinical like I'm being deprived of experiencing a fetus growing inside my own body, nourishing it into being a healthy baby within nine months, then giving birth, witnessing new life beautifully forcing its way out of my own. A biological miracle.

Although well-meaning, I do my best to absorb the barb about Hugh and how much he loves me because it's a painful reminder of my past relationships with Kyle and what happened with my college boyfriend Jordan. Two men who claimed to have loved me but clearly didn't.

She and I have been friends long enough for her to be around for all three which explains why she's firmly ensconced in Hugh's corner. I've come to her office to do more than have a heart to heart talk with her. I've come to use her computer, something I would've done at home had Kyle not started calling.

My job as an appraiser requires me to know the history of a parcel or dwelling and I know every back door program that allows me an inside look from the taxes the owner owes, to a quit claim deed that signals a couple is divorcing and are anxious to just get it sold, the proper building permits a structure might be lacking that will drive down sales, to how many times it has changed hands.

I look up the properties listed under Elise Davis's name. There are several ranging from an apartment building a couple miles east from downtown right on the border where the streets turn dangerous to a stretch of undeveloped land in Ojai, a chic little town full of Spanish architecture and rugged hills north of LA where celebrities like to snap up second homes and feel like they're living out in the country. Without seeing them, those two properties alone I'd appraise at eight figures each, at least fifteen million, maybe more.

At this rate of invaluable real estate, Elise might be wealthier than her late father.

Jessica leans over my shoulder. She's chewing

on a crunchy peeled carrot stick, watching her calories. I don't have to ask if she's still seeing her weekend boyfriend in the Bay area.

"What are you looking for?

I shrug.

"I'm not sure. I just know the cops are wasting time looking at me because her car was found in front of my house."

"You haven't done anything but show up to an appointment with dollar signs in your head like you always do."

"I know," I say, appreciating her support, however blunt it might be. "I don't know if they're looking anywhere else."

The front door opens.

"The police *should* be looking at that family of hers. What's left of them," she adds cheerily on her way out of the room.

Sometimes the harsh way things come out of Jessica's mouth makes it easy to understand why she's still single.

I hear her in the lobby speaking with her male secretary.

As I print out the pages listing Elise's numerous properties, it occurs to me that maybe my own focus has been too narrow. The notes aimed at me, her SUV burned to the ground at my house, all of it could be a distraction designed to throw off the cops.

Someone like Elise who has acquired so many assets all over Southern California and across half of the country could easily have made a few powerful enemies, investors or groups of investors in the form of shell corporations whom she outbid to get what she wanted or a deal gone bad. Things can turn ugly fast in her world. It isn't just property listings I should be looking for but also possible instances where she's fought somebody in court.

Chapter Twenty-One

~Back Then~

I REMEMBERED HARDLY DRINKING any alcohol, but somehow I felt drunk. Everything looked blurry at the edges, an unknown depth to each step I took. It made me afraid to move.

Rock music blared from the stereo down in the family room where Jordan's frat brothers were smoking weed and shouting over each other in the middle of a raucous drinking game. There'd be no way of cleaning the stench of marijuana out of the upholstery. My mother would smell it as soon as she returned home from her trip, a place I'd already forgotten but she'd left her itinerary, as she always did, under a magnet on the fridge in case I needed to contact her. She was still a mother even if she was rarely here with me anymore. The disappointment on her face knowing she couldn't trust me to be a responsible young adult would be a greater punishment than she could ever mete out.

As kids, in our old house in Toluca Lake, my father would sometimes move the furniture in the family room, clearing a space in the center. Then he'd turn on the radio and dance with Laney and me, exaggerated moves that made no sense and were completely out of sync with the beat of the music. Other times he'd sweep our mother in his arms and they'd sway and talk under their breaths to each other. The memory made me cry.

Jordan came up behind me and hooked his arm around my waist, pulling me closer to him. It wasn't a comforting embrace. I felt he was hard.

"There you are, Tia, Tia, Tia. Been looking all over for you."

Repeating my name made it sound like he'd been drinking heavily, but his voice sounded steady, no slurring. He kissed me roughly on the neck, a blood bruise in the form of a hickey I'd have to conceal for days with make-up. His kisses were never like that — meant to leave a physical mark on my skin. Something was different about him, something mean.

I tried to use my arm to gently push him back, giving me a little space. My attempt failed because I was too weak and I heard Jordan chuckle.

"I need some fresh air." It came out as a mumble I could hardly hear.

We were on the second floor. Family pictures on the wall spun around me and I was afraid I was about to pass out.

"No," Jordan whispered firmly. "You need to lie down…with me."

We were breaking up soon. I was breaking things off, once I found the right time and the nerve.

We hadn't had sex yet, at least not intercourse. My virginity was not sacred but it was mine. I no longer wanted Jordan to be the one to take it from me and I realized right then that he already knew all this.

We stood there at the top of the stairs. My knees felt as if they were about to give out yet Jordan kept me upright. Below us the party was going on, our friends *caught up in a good time fueled by alcohol and weed and plenty of hours of nighttime left. Their bodies became indistinguishable from one another, making me dizzier, and I blinked over and over, fighting hard for clarity that was already lost. If any of them looked up at Jordan and I standing there together, with both of his arms now wrapped around me, they'd think nothing of it. We were a couple after all. None of them would know how fast things had turned and that I was now being held against my will.*

CHAPTER TWENTY-TWO

BY MID-AFTERNOON I'M in a sleeveless black dress, matching leather flats, standing in front of Jordan's receptionist in the Assistant D.A.'s office downtown. I've also added a little mascara, some shiny color to my lips. Some might think I'm dressing up for my rapist, though that is far from my intention.

I can't tolerate him seeing me in any other condition than my very best.

My hair is a good twelve inches shorter than what he'll remember. Days after the night of the party I'd had it all chopped off – a perfect line at my neck. I had to appear to myself that I didn't look the same, that I'd started fresh. It was the only way I could stand seeing my reflection in the mirror.

I hated myself for allowing Jordan to make that stiff drink for me. And I hated that I stupidly let him pressure me into finishing it. I *hated* him for what he did to me afterwards.

Over the years there have been a couple of near run-ins, given he and I live in the same city, no matter how expansive the limits may be. There was the time Kyle's mother flew out here from her retirement home in Boca Raton to celebrate her son getting full tenure at UCLA. She was staying at a pricey hotel downtown and we'd just finished eating dinner at the restaurant on the rooftop. Jordan had entered the hotel lobby with a bunch of other suits just as Kyle and me were on the curb waiting for the valet to fetch the car. Jordan was caught up in conversation and hadn't given his surroundings a second glance.

Another time I'd been stopped at a traffic light and spotted him at a gas station on the corner, filling the tank of a fairly new Mercedes, his tie whipping up at him in the breeze. A blonde woman was in the passenger seat. All I could see was her profile and perfect posture. Though my eyes were focused on the intersection, I could sense the heat of someone staring at me, my mind playing jumpy tricks on me. As the light flicked green, I pressed hard on the gas, getting away as fast as I could.

"I don't have an appointment," I tell the woman once she finally looks up at me. "But I'd like to see Jordan if he's in." I swallow shards of glass to get this last part out. "I'm an old friend."

The woman looks me over, taking in "old friend" exactly how it sounds – a former lover or maybe she thinks I'm a current one. Either way I'm a complication she doesn't need when she must only have a couple hours left of her work day.

"What is your name?"

"Catia Wil – Catia Drakos," I say, using my maiden name.

She picks up the phone and calls into the office behind her with the two big stained wooden doors.

The son of a bitch is in.

He's inside that room several feet away.

Instinctively, I want to turn around, forgetting about the whole reason why I've come. His arms are around me again and he's slowing backing me away from the staircase, from our drunk friends downstairs who might put a stop to things if they only knew.

My mind goes blank after that clear memory.

I don't know what's worse – not knowing every place he invaded and violated me or being aware of every detail. In the morning I'd woken up alone with the inside of my thighs sore, a smattering of blood on the sheets. He'd raped me in what had once been my parents' bed. I was wearing nothing but my blouse I'd worn at the party, the buttoning wrong, and my bra was gone as if he'd redressed part of me instead of leaving me completely naked.

A minute passes as if Jordan is behind his desk in a fit, wondering how to get out of this, his dark past that has just tracked him down under the bright fluorescent lights of one of the largest prosecutor's offices in the country. Should he ignore me and tell his receptionist he's too busy to see me or ask me inside to hear why I've come to see him after all this time?

The woman nods, then hangs up.

"He'll see you, but he only has a few minutes. He has an important appointment."

Of course, he does. I bet she's quoting her boss word for word. The woman buzzes me in.

I take a deep breath, filling myself with the courage to walk in there and get what I want, what I need.

Jordan rounds his desk, the weighty version of him I'd watched the other night on TV contrasting with the lean younger guy I'd fallen head over heels for. They almost look like two different people.

"So good to see you again, Tia." His tone is friendly, a put on for his employee to hear before the door automatically closes behind me. "I have to say I'm a little surprised to see you after all this time, but it's wonderful you stopped by."

Had he not seen the news last night or read this morning's paper? Depending upon who you ask, I'm either a witness or a suspect to one of the biggest missing person's cases in his jurisdiction. But the Jordan I know is self-centered enough to only pay attention to the media if the news concerns him or he may stand to benefit from it. An underling might've mentioned to him Elise's car had been burned and abandoned at someone's home but that really isn't so uncommon. Killers dispose of evidence in remote places and if you didn't know my connection with Elise, the road I live on is about as desolate as any in the area.

On the shelf beside his desk is a framed photograph of two young girls, twins, in matching ruffled dresses. Their mother is young, much younger than Jordan. She is a brunette too. The blonde I'd seen in his car that day a faint memory. Jordan's young wife is in a pink shoulder-less dress and the way her long curls are arranged and the innocent smile on her face, I'm reminded of one of the underage princesses in the tournament of Roses Parade in Pasadena on New Year's Day.

I turn away because the picture disgusts me.

"I'm here about Elise Davis."

Jordan has a shocked expression. He sits back behind his desk.

"I can't go into the investigation, Tia."

"I didn't ask you to." My voice stuns me because it's strong, loaded with venom for this sick boy who grew up into a smug man who thinks he's gotten away with raping his former girlfriend with no repercussions.

He couldn't be more wrong.

That morning I woke up in an empty bed, my head felt like a block of cement I could barely lift up off the pillow. Once my feet were on the ground, I made my way out of the room on shaky legs as if I could collapse at any moment. Everyone from the party had gone home. Only the mess remained, beer bottles, dirty paper plates and pizza boxes on the tabletops and liquor stains on the carpets and upholstery. Jordan sat up on the couch in the family room when he saw me, then lifted up his hand in a flat waved hello. As I stood before him half-dressed, the way he'd left me, his eyes said it all. The coward didn't have the guts to sleep next me after what he'd done nor could he hardly look at me right then.

Being raped by a stranger is difficult enough to prove in the courts. Date rape is pretty much impossible. I couldn't report him to the university or go to the cops. Both of Jordan's parents were shrewd lawyers. They'd point out that he and I were dating and on this particular occasion we'd simply had too much to drink and things got out of hand. Both of us lost control of the situation. As added ammo, they'd point out I'd slept in the same room with their son under their very own roof.

So I did nothing except hack off my hair and break up with him.

I did nothing, but let it haunt the inner attic in my mind every time I lay intertwined in bed with Kyle and then later with Hugh.

For nearly two decades I did nothing, that is, until right now. My father suddenly comes to mind, the picture of the two of us on that sunny day posing in front of the Grand Canyon, in the exact place where some tourists have gotten too close to the edge and accidentally fell hundreds, even thousands of feet to their death with nothing to break their fall. My father hadn't wanted me to live in so much fear then. He wanted me to face it and realize I would be okay, if I used my common sense and stood on solid ground.

I blink away the memory and focus on the person seated across from me who's robbed me of ever loving any man freely with my whole heart. He owes me much more than the information I've come here to get.

"I need you to look into any sealed lawsuits she's settled and give me the names of those people she paid off."

Jordan shakes his head.

"You know I can't do that."

"You're running for mayor, right?"

I let my question fill the room with all of its implications. Rape may be hard to prove in the courts, but it's much easier to make the allegations known, no matter how long ago they may've occurred and let the public, the people of his constituency, decide for themselves.

Because of me, he could lose the election. He might even lose his entire career.

And Jordan knows this.

The flab around his neck where his skin is squeezed off by the neckline of his business shirt turns redder. His lips are wet from repeatedly licking them, a nervous habit he must've picked up along the way to the Assistant D.A.'s office.

"And how do I know you'll keep your mouth shut if I give you the names."

I look him square in the eyes because that's what someone with the upper hand does.

"You don't."

"Fuck you, Tia."

Jordan is absolutely enraged, frustrated that he's being blackmailed by his own grave moral mistakes. But he suddenly gets up and storms out of the office.

Finally, I have a seat in one of the chairs on the opposite side of his desk, the blood restoring to all my extremities. I've never stood up to anyone in my life like I did just now and I'm changed in a way I don't fully recognize yet.

Less than ten minutes later Jordan returns with

a print out with two case numbers and two plaintiff's names on it, a woman who was paid an undisclosed amount last year for her beach-front property in Pacific Palisades and a man who worked as a building manager of one of the apartment building's Elise owned, the one I noticed earlier at Jessica's office as being prime real estate, sitting on the border between wealth and poverty. The man received the sum of money less than three months ago and is still residing in the building.

Each of these two people has a story about Elise, one that she went to the lengths of the law to keep secret, one that I doubt Detective Ramirez or his partner has uncovered yet.

"This is it," Jordan demands as if he has a choice. "It ends here. I won't be extorted by you again."

But I hear the worry in his voice way more than I do the tough talk. He's just shown me his hand and it's a vulnerable one.

I raise my own hand and give him the same open-handed wave he gave me that morning he slept on the couch – a handshake of sorts, a begrudging pact between two fiercely opposed people who understand what the other is capable of.

For once *he is helpless*. The court of public opinion can be far more ruthless than any court of law. His livelihood hinges on my silence. He is at my mercy and there is nothing else Jordan can do but watch me leave his office and hope I don't come back.

CHAPTER TWENTY-THREE

IN THE PARKING lot, with the engine running, I turn on my phone to input the directions of the two addresses of the people Elise paid off. Instantly, all of my messages pop up, a clutter of names and telephone numbers blocking my plans. One message and four recent calls are from Kyle. Reluctantly, I play the message back, preparing for the outrage at violating Becca's privacy, his voice volcanic.

I can hear it now.

I'm the one acting like a stalker.

Instead he seems subdued, a reminder call that I still haven't appraised the Encino home. His tone sounds worried. He lingers on the line a few seconds like he wants to say more but isn't sure how to articulate it.

I'd been married to him long enough to read his silence.

He has heard about Elise's SUV destroyed by ash and flames practically at my doorstep. He has no clue yet that I've used his password to hack into his girlfriend's academic records or that I called around and found out she's a violent lunatic. Another call is from Detective Ramirez, but it's cut off from an incoming one marked "home."

Someone is calling me from my own landline.

I think of the new locks on the front and back doors that were installed this morning. I was handed a shiny new key. But it's just that, a key.

A window could easily be smashed in.

The press is gone and my neighbors live far enough away not to hear anything much less see anybody suspicious. For a split second, I panic. Has the same person who set fire to Elise's SUV broken in and is now inside my own home, letting me know I'm about to lose everything?

All of my precious belongings – my wedding photo album with Kyle, pictures of the two of us in our own new private world during our first dance as husband and wife or the one of my sister Laney and her spouse ridiculously dancing in a Conga line comprised of just the two of them. It's a rare moment where my sister has been caught relaxed from alcohol and joy, willing to let herself have an openly good time. Why hadn't I ever thought to transfer the pictures to the computer for safekeeping? And there's my father's record player with the delicate needle I've kept in mint condition and still play jazz and Motown music on – everything that means anything to me gone.

I click on my phone to take the call.

"Tia, you need to come home."

It's Hugh. He's the one in my house.

The locksmith had given me one key. There is always a spare made yet I'd been so preoccupied with getting back to finding out about Becca's past that I hadn't thought to ask. Hugh must've arranged to be given the other key which irks me. After our big fight yesterday, he shouldn't feel like he's on such solid ground.

"I really can't," I say, because I have the directions of the two addresses ready to go on my phone.

There's at least another hour or so of daylight left. I might be able to talk with at least one of the two people who'd been angry enough with Elise to pursue their rights in court. Calling them on the phone is pointless. The files had been sealed which means they are barred from talking about the case or the settlement.

I'm taking a risk as it is that either of them will speak to me in person. They definitely won't risk speaking with me on the phone.

"You need to," Hugh demands. "When I got here a little while ago a TV crew was setting up all their equipment. None of them get that they're trespassing. Nobody's listening to a god-damn word I'm saying. The Davis Family is here too. They're insisting on giving their first tele-vised interview here at the house."

They're still filming by the time I get home and I'm told by a young kid who looks like a band roadie to please park down the road *from my own house.* Five director chairs are set up a few feet from my porch, right beside the black-ened splotch where Elise's SUV burned so hot it made the gravel turn color. Collected off to the side, away from the view of the cameras, stand a few behind-the-scenes production people and a skinny collapsible table with make-up and hair products.

Seeing Elise's family members all aligned next to one another in front of the backdrop that is my home, I'm reminded of a group of cast members on a set chatting to an entertainment reporter about their latest film.

Gia sits pretty nearest the male host, a real journalist for this particular network who only gets called in to cover the serious one-hour specials. She dabs at her eyes with a pale blue handkerchief that matches the color of her dress. Glamour over grief – I suddenly resent her even more. A woman who claims to have loved her estranged husband wouldn't focus on herself down to the detail of the color of fabric she'll be seen by the public crying with.

I don't know why she's here. This is about Elise, not her father. Given her age, Gia hardly looks like the concerned stepmother, though that doesn't mean she and Elise couldn't have a close relationship. I could've been all wrong judging her so swiftly that day in her boutique.

Considering I heard Deborah compare Gia's worth to a box of fruit the other day, Elise, too, probably saw this woman as a calculated opportunist, waiting out her time. While wealth and celebrity may draw a striking much younger woman like Gia, it doesn't change the reality Carson was far too old for any real future to be had between them.

On the other side of Gia is Edward in a khaki colored suit with no tie, then the meticulous gray bearded lawyer and at the far end is Deborah. As Elise's wife, she should be the one sitting closest to the host. It appears like she wants to stay as far away from this scene and still be a part of it as she can.

At one point the host refers to her as Dr. Landon, her maiden name.

There's a question for her, too, that she reluctantly answers. Approximately how long she and Elise have known each other, sharing this intimate detail about their relationship they'd fought so hard to keep private with an audience of millions. But then her eyes drift somewhere else again, not on the host nor Edward who is rattling off the number of a tip line.

The reward for Elise is now at two million, a sum high enough to complicate things with false leads or unrelated suspects.

Detective Ramirez can't be happy about this.

Edward's expression is confident. He has a quick command of the camera like his father and there is no stopping him. After the interview airs, if he has any social media accounts, he'll gain thousands of followers. Something tells me Edward is completely unplugged from technology and that what I'm watching is a fine performance from a man with acting in his blood.

"She's my only sibling," he explains to the host. Briefly, he looks to the others lined up beside him. "We *all* want her back. The police are doing what they can, but the public is nearly always quicker at solving crimes and finding people."

The sky is growing dark and the surrounding

lights set up to illuminate the Davis Family make it seem like they're the center of their own special universe.

In a way they are.

But even all their money and their late patriarch's legendary status can't keep them from being another victimized family pleading with the public for help because the investigators are apparently all out of leads.

Hugh appears right out of the shadows in front of me and takes me in his arms.

"I'm sorry," he says softly, which could refer to either him lying to me about being sterile at the beginning of our relationship or the situation with the Davis Family playing out before us that he couldn't prevent.

I wrap my arms around his waist. He smells freshly showered, the back of his T-shirt a little damp because he has a bad habit of never fully drying off. Jessica might be right. The vasectomy reversals do work most of the time. He did have the procedure done not too long after he realized how badly I want a baby. We can get past this. I can go with Hugh to his doctor and be reassured by the strong odds. We still can make a baby. Not many men his age would go through so much to try and start a second family.

And here I am carrying on a grudge because he went under the knife shortly after meeting me in order to reverse the course of his life and become a father again. How much of my anger towards Hugh is really about him not telling me the truth? Deep inside I've never been able to fully trust any man. Laney could be right. That night, all those years before, when we argued in the kitchen after Jordan had come for dinner, she'd predicted that not getting over our father's death would leave me vulnerable in ways I couldn't understand. She'd seen something destructive about Jordan that I was blinded to. Now I find myself about to force a good man out of my life.

"After this interview airs, your place might become a new creepy hangout for drunk teenagers," Hugh warns.

I pull back a little so our eyes meet.

"Only if Elise had been killed here," I point out. I keep my voice low so we don't interfere with the taping. "People care about the murdered, not so much about the missing. Just because her SUV was destroyed, it doesn't mean she's dead. I don't blame her family for what they're doing. They're trying to get the public's attention. There could be a witness who might come forward. Or her abductor will be watching."

Hugh looks a little stunned.

"You think there's a possibility someone saw the person who came here and set fire to her car?"

"Maybe. Whoever it was might have an accomplice that's getting scared enough to talk. Another car had to be arranged and left nearby to make a quick getaway. Though it could be just one clever person who's carefully planned out everything."

Hugh acts like this is the first he's thought about there being more than one person behind Elise's disappearance. But he's a smart man and this possibility has no doubt already crossed his mind. He's the one behind the changed locks after all.

"You haven't found a note today?"

"No."

We both know that means very little and there's the real possibility another one could show up the next morning in a new place like taped, without a trace, to the front door of the house.

The interview is wrapping up. Someone has let themselves into my home and flipped on the porch light. The director chairs are being folded up and the backlighting is being taken down.

Gia is standing close, flirting with the host. Maybe as a former flight attendant she can't turn off her female charms.

My criticism of her might come from envy.

My height, my large eyes and small chest make me feel out of balance, awkward in my own skin. When men give me attention I don't know what they're staring at – my better features or my flaws.

Hugh goes on ahead of me to make sure the TV crew leaves in a timely manner.

A woman who I hadn't noticed before holds Edward's hand. She'd been standing off to the side with the production crew. A simple beauty, petite, with straight brown hair, dark skin and a fresh innocent face that has little to do with her age but more about the kind of clean life she's lead. She must be one of the main reasons why he's remained in Nepal.

Edward lights up with her touch. They're clearly romantically involved and he loves her.

"Edward's girlfriend flew in earlier today," explains Deborah.

She kisses my cheek as if we are friends or allies – in a way I guess we are. Both of us find ourselves on the outside of the Carson Davis Family's inner circle. Somehow Carson's estranged wife whom he was in the process of divorcing holds more clout than Elise's wife. Between her and Edward, they'd dominated the interview, answering most of the questions. Even the lawyer who's used to speaking up because of his profession couldn't get in much more than a nod. Deborah seated at the farthest end from the interviewer might not have been by choice.

Nevertheless, Elise would be proud of how well her wife is holding up in her absence. Deborah introduces me to the gray bearded lawyer from an expensive sounding firm in Beverly Hills. He's also a family friend, a former golfing buddy of Carson's. I get the feeling he forgets my name as soon as Deborah tells him. His sympathy and time are strictly spared for the family members. While not exactly the spokesperson for the family, he has to be the executor of Carson's will, the way he's taken an active part in the vigil and this nationwide interview.

I bet he's the one instrumental in pulling off the elaborate move of changing Carson's place of death from a hospital bed in his home in Bel Air to the choppy waters of the Atlantic off the coast of Spain. A death far more befitting of Hollywood royalty. What exactly would it take? Access to a private jet? A few people paid off to orchestrate the boating accident? How hard would it be to get the coroner in that small coastal town to rule Carson's death a drowning even if there is no water in his lungs? What if he was paid off to sign the autopsy *without ever seeing the body*?

It's my understanding, upon recovering Carson's body, it was immediately cremated. But that's something I caught on the news and after the family pulled off Carson's made up statement to the press shortly after Elise went missing, they're capable of getting away with just about anything.

The lawyer must also know the contents of Carson's will, the last time it's been updated, whether it's been this past year or not in five. The way Gia is hanging around, appearing heartbroken, makes it seem like she thinks she's still very much in it. Maybe she and the lawyer are sleeping together. After she says her goodbyes to the TV host, she walks over to the lawyer's Lexus and gets inside. The two of them drove here together.

Deborah waits until the lawyer joins Gia in his car before she brings up what happened here yesterday.

"I don't know why someone would do that to you. Leave Elise's BMW in front of your house in that condition." She says this not like she suspects me of anything but as if she's trying to figure it out herself. "When the police first called and told me I was afraid she'd been locked inside and was burning alive." She pauses to take a breath. "I made them repeat it to me twice that she wasn't."

Deborah doesn't ask about the notes.

I find it hard to believe Edward wouldn't tell

her about them. Maybe he's decided not to because she's pregnant and has enough to worry about with her wife missing or the graphic image she's come up with of her wife burning to death might've made her temporarily forget everything else.

"Did Detective Ramirez or his partner cooperate and do an interview?" I ask.

Deborah rolls her eyes.

"The two of them, they claim they're too busy following new leads. More like following each other's tails. They've found *nothing. They tell me nothing.*"

I think back to the night of the vigil and how she and Detective Ramirez were deep in conversation. Things could've rapidly changed since then though it seems unlikely.

Edward catches my eye and lifts his chin, a friendly gesture. His demeanor is different, more relaxed. The woman by his side must be the reason, a reminder of his obscure life a world away from the celebrity fishbowl he finds himself looking out of, a place with dirt floor villages, sudden pounding rains, honored traditions *and her.* The media at his beck and call, his late father's lavish mansion in Bel Air and immense wealth that could buy him virtually anything he wants except the one thing he wants most of all which is to return back to the geographical roots he's dug for himself far away from here in Nepal.

I wave back, relieved to acknowledge him without us having to actually talk to one another. Who knows how long his good nature will last before he starts in on me again this time with questions about my possible connection with Elise's abductor? How could I convince him that I don't know anything more than he does?

"When will it air?" I ask Deborah.

"Tomorrow night. This goddamn family of hers." Deborah's voice is a hard whisper, almost loud enough for the rest of them to hear. "Elise was never allowed to be her own person. She was the one who took care of her father. There was never any other choice." Deborah stops short of bringing up his declining health or confessing to me about the hospital bed and the respirator we both know was keeping him alive. "And now, they keep claiming they desperately need to know what happened to her, but all they're really concerned with is that her being gone is holding up the reading of the will."

I listen because I don't think she has anyone else to confide in, yet I can't help but notice. The one person who should be clinging most to the hope that Elise might still be alive is referring to her in the past tense as if she is already dead.

CHAPTER TWENTY-FOUR

IN THE MORNING I drive off at the same time as Hugh, promising I'll meet him for lunch at Canter's on Fairfax, a promise I don't intend to keep. He's still uneasy about leaving me home alone and lunch is a means of keeping tabs on me. I've told him I'm looking at some properties for work; I neglected to mention the connection the two people I'm going to see have with Elise. If I do, I'm worried he'll pressure me to drop my plans and call the police and let them follow up or, out of concern, he might go behind my back and notify Detective Ramirez with the information himself.

Traffic lightens leaving L.A. while on the other side of the 210 Freeway commuters inch in from the suburbs. I'm heading in the direction of the address of the older woman who once owned the property in Pacific Palisades. She now lives in Pasadena. Because she's sixty-seven, I assume she's retired and will be home at this time, mid-morning.

It's a pleasant street she lives on with landscaped yards of grass that roll out over the front yard like carpet, blooming rose bushes and wooden fences separating one house from the next. Property in this area starts in the mid six figures, an upper middle-class neighborhood with very little crime. It doesn't change the fact her current home won't remotely compare with her former beachfront residence looking out over the Pacific, and when I get to the address, it most certainly doesn't. It's a modest two-bedroom, white clapboard with black trim framing the windows. A couple sprinklers tick out water in the front.

I knock on the brick red door. A Nissan four door is parked in the driveway, so I'm assuming she's home.

In the seconds waiting for her to open the door, I feel like I'm being watched. This is the kind of neighborhood where the people that live here report back to one another, the comings and goings of their fellow neighbors. Anyone new might raise an eyebrow. An unofficial nosy neighborhood watch group.

At least this is what I'm hoping.

Elise's abductor hadn't left a note for me this morning, but that doesn't mean another one isn't about to show up on my car or I will be startled to the bone in some other kind of way. Things are ramping up, the danger palpable that for whatever reason I am in the crosshairs. It's been nearly two days since I found the Post-It note on the mirror in the women's restroom at the restaurant. That note had been a warning – I was about to get the shock of my life, racing towards the biggest piece of evidence in Elise's disappearance as it was being destroyed by uncontrolled flames right at my very own house. Had the person been hidden in the brush nearby, relishing in the fear on my face that my friend was burning alive and I could do nothing? What else did this sick person have in store for me?

The bolt on the other side of the door slides and soon I'm staring at a young woman with a stringy dirty blond ponytail, in yoga pants, a tank top and a sheen of sweat on her neck. Her kickass body is enviably lean and muscled. She eyes my casual outfit, flat sandals, curiously.

"You look familiar," she says, and I worry she might recognize the footage of me being driven off in the back of Detective Ramirez's car the other day.

I don't want to give her the chance to remember and blow right past her comment.

"I'm sorry for bothering you, but I'm looking for Mrs. Keaton."

"That's my mother. What's this about?"

I'm prepared to get the door slammed in my face.

"Elise Davis."

The woman turns the knob hard in her hand, the name giving her pause. Her face is unreadable as she stands at the door undecided what to do.

Mrs. Keaton's daughter is physically strong, the kind that must teach exercise classes, not necessarily meditation yoga or dance but hand-to-hand survival techniques for women, maybe boxing. No man could get the drop on her.

She might easily be able to sneak up on another woman from behind as she got out of her car, roughly push her back in, muffling her victim's mouth, then drive away cleanly.

"My mom's at work," she finally says. "Simpson's Market on Colorado Boulevard. Two blocks and then make a right."

As I drive to the grocery store, I check the rearview mirror and see no cars that are recognizable. If someone is following me, I doubt I'd know what car it would be anyway. I don't even know what kind of car Becca drives.

I am surprised someone Mrs. Keaton's age is working anywhere, much less in such a physically active position. She was widowed not that long ago and I imagine her husband must've left her his pension and then there's his social security too and the undisclosed settlement money the courts forcibly made Elise give her. It doesn't make sense.

Once inside the grocery store I'm directed by an employee to an aisle where a woman with short white hair and bangs brushed to one side is stocking soup cans on a shelf. The closer I get, she smiles at me before returning to her work.

As soon as I introduce myself and tell her why I'm here, her friendly smile stops. She is not so much as angry at Elise as she is petrified by her.

"How did you find me? All of that is supposed to be sealed."

"It is," I reassure her, though that doesn't explain how I've found her. "Please. I just want to know what happened to your home in Pacific Palisades. Why did she have to settle with you? What went wrong?"

She turns towards the tomato bisque cans she's just neatly arranged. She is crying and I hate myself for pressing an old widow to relive something so painful she thought was in the past.

I touch her shoulder, and she hunches forward, the story behind her court battle with Elise physically weakening her even more just by being reminded of it.

"I lived in that home with my husband Charles for thirty-nine years. We raised our daughter there." She turns and looks at me. "You must've just met her."

I nod.

Mrs. Keaton continues.

"The money my husband left me wasn't enough to keep up with the payments so I decided to do a reverse mortgage with the bank. I filled out the paperwork. It was notarized right in front of me at the bank." She shakes her head. "I know it was. Everything was in order. Then a couple weeks later someone shows up at my door and informs me I have thirty days to vacate the premises. That's what he called *my home,* "the premises.""

I don't understand.

"What happened to the bank papers?"

Mrs. Keaton shrugs.

"They were never filed. They used my age against me, said I was batty and forgetful. I hadn't filed anything with them. If it wasn't for my daughter…well, my Claudia stirred things up at the bank. She threatened to report them to the government, claiming they intentionally lost my paperwork for the reverse mortgage so the land could be bought for next to nothing by one of their best clients, Elise Davis. That's how we found out it was Ms. Davis. Claudia filed a lawsuit against her and then Ms. Davis's attorneys stepped in and wanted to settle."

While Jordan had gotten me a printout of the two cases Elise settled and had sealed, the amount of money Mrs. Keaton and the man named Marcus O'Brien settled for were not listed. Jordan covered his ass as best he could.

"May I ask how much Elise paid you?"

Mrs. Keaton sighs.

"Two hundred and fifty thousand."

My heart sinks, my appraiser's mind setting the value of her former home, sight unseen, in Pacific Palisades well into the millions. What Elise cheated this woman out of is absolutely criminal and yet legal in the blurred boundaries of her real estate world where the banks are at her disposal.

Mrs. Keaton's eyes well with tears again and she wipes them with the back of her fragile hand, the skin paper thin and marked by veins that are the color of a newly made bruise. Her wedding band is still on her left ring finger.

"That's why I got this job. In such a small place with my late husband's pension and Claudia moving in, pitching in on the bills, I could afford to stay home. But I can hardly stand being in that place. It only reminds me of all the memories I've lost. I used to be able to walk into the kitchen and see the markings on the wall of Claudia as a small child growing up, inch by inch, or the oil stains on the floor in the garage from my husband's late model Thunderbird he'd leisurely drive around on Sundays."

This is not the Elise I know. This one is unscrupulous and very cruel.

Mrs. Keaton has every right to wish the worst for Elise.

Instead she shares with me that she sincerely wishes the police find her because her family, they must be worried sick. Then Mrs. Keaton turns away, forgetting about the work she's left unfinished, a shelf half-stocked with split pea soup, and she quickens her pace down the aisle until I lose sight of her around the corner.

I call Hugh on my way to the second address, backing out on our lunch plans at Canter's. The next job I'm going to is going to take longer than I expected I explain and because I'm a freelance appraiser there's no reason to not buy my excuse.

Hugh is quiet on the other end, no doubt checking himself because we're getting along better now since I've made the decision to stop resenting him for not telling me about his vasectomy he'd had while married to Carolyn. He's back in my bed and he doesn't want to blow it.

"Please promise me you won't be anywhere alone. There's a reason why that woman's car was left to burn in front of your house. Some sadistic son of a bitch might want to take you next."

I'm not a hundred percent sure it's a man behind all this the way Hugh clearly is, but I've also yet to tell him about Becca crushing a woman's mouth with a tire iron either. I've told no one, not even Jessica or Laney. It's something I definitely need to tell Detective Ramirez about and I will when I finally return his call even if it leaves a trail back to me calling, under false pretenses, a faculty member and classmate from her former university and hacking into her academic records.

I make a promise to Hugh I know that I can't keep, then I hang up.

In between Pasadena and Los Angeles, I pick up a greasy cheeseburger, fries and a soda in a fast food drive thru, spooked that if I go inside to eat I may come out to the Prius with four slashed tires or a shattered windshield.

The man I'm about to see, Marcus O'Brien, is in his fifties and worked as an apartment manager for Elise's building. From what I've gathered he doesn't hold a second job and is on disability.

Traffic builds the closer I get to downtown. Next to the freeway is the beige colored prison with its coiled barbed wire and slivered windows that tease the prisoners with an ounce of daylight. A mixture of messy and artful graffiti and murals depicting real faces of humanity cover every inch of the concrete sides of the freeway.

Real estate investors continue to tear down tenements in the immediate proximity of the skyscrapers downtown and replace them with high rise condominiums for wealthy professionals, pushing out the poor and the homeless. I turn on Spring Street and drive a couple blocks east of downtown where the strip malls thin out and low-income residences crop up.

I pull into the three-story apartment complex that once looked like it had been a cheery, colorful place to live. Where there once appeared to be bushes and flowers rooted in the dirt next to the sidewalk, there is upturned earth as if someone took a shovel and dug them all up. Chalk outlines for hopscotch mark the sidewalk signaling young children used to live here.

Only a couple of cars are parked in the lot. Even at this time of day there should be more. I'd read about this place when I was on the computer at Jessica's office. Recently, the residents of this building received a notice to vacate as there were plans for it to be demolished in the coming weeks.

Further inside the courtyard I glimpse a drained pool, cluttered with leaves and debris where I'm sure the children who'd drawn with chalk on the sidewalk spent plenty of time splashing and playing in the pool.

Marcus O'Brien lives on the first floor nearest the rows upon rows of locked residents' mailboxes. He is a black man with a bum shoulder he injured working at a warehouse in his thirties. When he answers the door in a dark gray t-shirt and work coveralls, I see in every other aspect he appears to be a strong man for his age. By what he's wearing it's as if it hasn't fully registered he no longer has to do his job anymore. I'm sure he could still crawl under a sink and fix a leaky faucet using his good arm or bang on another tenant's door if things inside were getting too rowdy.

After hearing about why I'm here, he doesn't ask me to leave like I'm anticipating. Instead he lets me inside and offers me a cup of coffee from a pot that looks like it's been sitting there since this morning.

I take him up on his offer anyway because he's showing me such courtesy. Just like Mrs. Keaton he doesn't appear to be a bad person.

Dirty plates and glasses are heaped up in the sink, too many it seems to have come from just one person. The rest of the apartment looks fairly tidy.

"You live alone?" I ask.

"My wife is a perfume manager at Macy's," he explains. "Commutes all the way to Santa Monica from here. Between the drive and the overtime hours, I hardly ever see her."

Marcus sits across from me at the kitchen table and takes a sip of the coffee, nearly spitting it out.

"That shit's thick," he apologizes. "Let me make a fresh pot."

I laugh.

"It's okay," I say. "I'm still trying to digest my cheeseburger and fries I ate on the way over here."

"You know I'm not supposed to talk about the settlement."

"I know," I say. I decide to be candid with him because I don't think he'll tell me anything if I'm not. "Her SUV she was last seen in was left burning on my property. We were friends…back when we were kids," I add, doing what I can to distance myself from Elise, remembering she is kicking this man out of his own home.

Marcus leans back and turns the mug on the table.

"Once she decided she was going to have this place torn down, she stopped paying me. She said my disability checks covered my expenses. I'd be alright."

"But that money was owed to you. There were still tenants here, right?"

"There's still a few left. We stay out of each other's way. I think we're all staying as long as we can until the bulldozers pull up because we need to save first and last month's rent for a new place."

"That's understandable."

"My wife has a brother who's a lawyer and he filed the papers and we took her to court. She claimed to the judge she'd fired me months ago. Even shared with the court a phony termination letter she never sent me just to cover her own ass."

He lets out a loud whistle that is wired with menace.

"That bitch thinks of everything."

"How were you able to get any money out of her?"

"My brother-in-law told her in the halls during the courtroom break that he was going to the papers." Marcus shrugs. "He could've gotten in deep trouble if she'd said anything to the judge. Unprofessional and all. She quickly changed her tune, though the amount wasn't much for her. Fifteen grand."

Marcus appears oddly calm as if he's fully accepted things as they are because he knows he cannot change them.

If word got out about Elise's real estate dealings she treated like a blood sport, it would not only deeply hurt her reputation as a businesswoman but her father's celebrity name as well. Other family members or people close to them like the meticulous gray bearded lawyer, would most likely never allow that, which is why, on the rare occasions she was caught, she inevitably broke out the checkbook, then had her mistakes permanently sealed from public view by the courts.

This Elise Davis, the one who robs from a widow and cheats a man on disability, is a stranger to me. In less than six hours, after hearing Mrs. Keaton and Marcus's stories, my entire friendship with Elise has suffered damage beyond repair.

CHAPTER TWENTY-FIVE

THE CHARITY ELISE apparently runs on her father's behalf for children with heart disease aside, it is the brutal way in which she conducts her own business affairs that could easily make her a target of someone's rage. Detective Ramirez and his partner might not be looking in the right places. *Where are they even looking?* Last night Deborah sounded like they weren't telling her much. They weren't even allowing themselves to be interviewed for the special that airs tonight.

I've put off returning Detective Ramirez's call. If he wants me to come back to the station and be interviewed again, this time I'll decline.

I'm not a suspect and I'm tired of feeling like one, especially under his female partner's glare. Detective Ramirez may not outright be accusing me of anything, but I sense he thinks things about my life aren't as they seem.

After speaking with Mrs. Keaton and Marcus, I'm hesitant to volunteer their names to the police for further investigation.

They are her victims.

Besides, a part of me doesn't want Detective Ramirez getting curious, questioning me about how I obtained their names from sealed court documents.

There is something empowering about knowing I have forced Jordan to jeopardize his job as Assistant District Attorney as well as his entire political future for me and that I could do it again.

I know the side streets well enough so I get off the Venture Freeway early. I can't shake the feeling I'm being followed, and I take another look in the rear-view mirror, not sure of what I'm looking for.

To begin with, I don't know what type of car Becca drives, if in fact she's the one behind all this. I think of the girl she beat with a tire iron. If she could do that to her new girlfriend's lover, what might she be capable of doing to a nosy ex-wife? Should she find out that I've dug into her past she might mistakenly think I want Kyle back. I realize I've told no one about Becca shattering that poor girl's jaw, not Jessica or even Hugh.

It might not even be Becca who's doing this to me, so I slow down when someone tails my car too closely and try and get a good look through the rear-view mirror at the driver to see if I recognize the face of the person behind the wheel. So far, I've come up with nothing, visors pulled down that cut off telling facial features and my own blinding glare from the sunlight.

After a couple traffic lights, I'm winding up a steep incline into the hills in Encino. The engine of the Prius becomes gutless and I press harder on the gas, afraid it might suddenly roll backwards.

The neighborhood is strangely quiet like it's missing all the people who must live here. There are no children out front playing even though most schools have let out for the day by this time in the afternoon. I make a mental note that this neighborhood is probably made up of older professionals still at their jobs. Custom built homes, almost all sprawling one stories, are set deep off the road as if hiding out among the oak and eucalyptus trees that shadow the street. My place, although so removed from other homes, is perfect for a child to be raised in and play.

My borderless property provides plenty of room for a swing set, a trampoline. There'd never be any need to go to a public park unless my child wanted to socialize with other kids. My eyes fill up the way they always do when I picture my life the way it should be, as a loving mother packing school lunches of healthy almond butter sandwiches and fruit roll-ups, and I can't help at times like this but feel the loss. The absence, it can be excruciating and it does not matter what man I love is sharing the rooms in my house with me because I am still, in so many ways, naturally abandoned.

The automated voice on my GPS lets me know the house I'm supposed to appraise is less than one mile away.

Out of nowhere, a kid on a bicycle cuts across the street right in front of my bumper, and I brake hard narrowly avoiding hitting him. Scared, the boy stops too, realizing he could've been run over. He looks about eleven, maybe twelve and under the shade of the trees his hands on the handle bars of his bike seem discolored.

Once he regains his breath, he spins his bike in the other direction and pedals down a side street.

As I approach the paved circular driveway, Glen's Tesla, a black Range Rover and brand new white Porsche Carrera with a temporary paper license plate, make their way out in a caravan of luxury vehicles.

Glen puts down his window and raises his arm.

I wave back, happy for once to see him.

The fact they've just left the house eases my mind. I am in for no surprises once I get inside – no cryptic notes or a person hiding behind a door or in a closet, waiting to take their game of toying with me to another level. It's not uncommon for realtors to get the jump on a property before it's been appraised and listed on the market.

I unscramble the combination on the lockbox hanging off the doorknob and use the key inside to unlock the front door. The home is bare, unfurnished. Seventies style wood paneling darkens the rooms but the carpet is a plush creamy off white. I make sure to bolt the front door locking myself inside the empty house before I get to work.

In the kitchen I turn on the light and snap pictures with my phone of the Formica countertop, the linoleum, the color of egg yolks, the stainless-steel fridge. The house appears as if the owners were in the process of updating it before giving up and deciding to sell.

The house is too quiet and secluded, and the confidence I'd had of people being in here before me is starting to wane.

They are all gone now, and I am alone.

If I'm right about somebody following me, now is the chance to ambush me. My screams could easily be muffled and the eight- foot high stucco wall separating this property from the next will be impossible for me to climb should I make it outside and try to scale it. The neighbor probably isn't even home.

I move faster though the three small bedrooms, the air stale, unlived in. Then I am in the much larger master bedroom and bath with an oval shaped tub, a walk-in closet I decide not to enter. A cracking sound comes from the corner of the ceiling and startles me.

Adrenaline shoots like lightning through my limbs. I've heard that sound countless times before, the sound of a house settling, though my heart is pounding in my chest.

I need out of here now, but I tell myself I'm nearly finished.

All that is left for me to do is take pictures of the backyard and the pool and I can get in my car and drive away.

Outside a breeze moves the branches of the large trees overhead. The pool is littered with leaves and a layer of dirt, unused for quite some time, but still filled up to the decorative tiles along the edge, apparently tended to on occasion. I snap a picture of the skinny diving board.

A few yards back beyond the pool, nearly obscured by the longer spidery strands of two weeping willows, sits a pool house I'm not expecting. I walk closer to the double French doors and take a picture. I try one of the doorknobs but it's locked. Given Glen's impatient nature, I doubt he took the time to fully examine the pool house, if he came out here at all. They probably toured the home and looked out at the pool from inside the house.

Kyle will be pleased I'm now estimating the price of this property at half a million. A key starter home for a TV producer cutting his or her teeth in Hollywood or a surgeon from one of the better hospitals in the area with a young family, a home that can be remodeled one room to the next while still being able to live in it.

Next to the door of the pool house, something that at first glance looks like a sweeping decorative design is on the wall. I have to take a step back to fully see that it's not a design at all, but oversized lower-case letters. They are fuzzy from the spray paint used, two words in a cold blue, caught in mid-drip on the wood.

I do not have a chance to heed the warning and turn around. The blow is sudden, it's sharp, and I see nothing but a blinding white light before I hit the ground.

———◆———

The first thing I feel is an unbearable pain that feels like I shouldn't try and move my head. Then when I open my eyes, I see a blurry white curtain that seems to be moving in a breeze. But that's impossible because I'm in a room, an emergency room. My back is propped up at an angle and two metal bedrails are on either side of me. I'm still in my own clothes.

Kyle leans forward, his dark bangs in the way, like he's been anticipating me to wake up for some time.

The fluorescent lights overhead hurt my eyes and I turn my head, the wrong way, towards him. Suddenly I feel nauseous.

"What are you doing here?"

He's smiling as if that's not the question he's expecting me to ask.

I guess I should be asking what happened.

"Glen called to let me know he'd shown the property to some other realtors. He mentioned he saw you as they were leaving, so I tried calling your cell. You didn't pick up. I began to worry."

Glen? When did the two of them become friendly enough to share a personal call about me? But then I realize it has little to do with me. It's just business and Kyle will talk to anyone, no matter how much he can't stand them, if it means a big commission and an even bigger name for himself.

He studies my hand, the needle taped to it, sticking out from the top with the tiny tube feeding me fluids intravenously. He lifts the underside of my palm delicately, then he turns his eyes away to keep me from seeing him cry.

The only time I remember him crying in front of me is when his college friend died from a drug overdose. They'd lost touch. Kyle had become a success while his friend turned into a failure, a lost job, a disgusted wife who left him and an expensive addiction to coke. Kyle felt guilt too, because when his friend called out of the blue, weeks earlier, asking for a loan, Kyle blew him off. Instead of showing up to the funeral, Kyle sent flowers because he didn't want anyone to see him so emotionally worked up, so goddamn weak.

"Fuck, Tia," he says, miserably. He still loves me deeply. I can hear it in his voice. "You could've been killed."

I fight for clarity, to put together what happened — somebody struck me from behind. I reach back and touch the source of my throbbing pain, a thin strip of clean-shaven scalp and a row of ridged sutures at the base of my head.

Dried blood.

My head was split right open.

Kyle gently guides my arm back to my chest.

"Don't worry, the rest of your hair covers it. You needed six stitches," he tells me. "They did a CT scan and you're going to be okay. You've suffered a mild concussion. It's remarkable, really. The doctors aren't certain what you were hit with."

He won't stop talking and he starts to lose focus or maybe I am.

The pain is so intense I regret that I came to. Kyle's features come in at me like they're three dimensional, his eyes first, then the rest of his face. He's a dizzying puzzle I can't piece together, so I look away. My stomach feels sick like I could throw up.

This much I remember. Someone had been following me and that person distracted me with the words painted on the wall in order to hit me with something so hard I was knocked unconscious.

"I called that detective working on Elise's case." Kyle is talking again. "He's on his way over."

My eyes are still closed because it helps with the nausea that comes up, then subsides in unrelenting waves.

"How do you know him?"

Kyle laughs though it's empty of any humor.

"That old pit bull came over to my place and grilled me, he grilled Becca too. We were forced to produce alibis for the other day when Elise's car was set on fire at your house, which, you know, we did."

Becca.

Knocking someone out cold with a blunt instrument is similar to shattering their jaw.

It's only a matter of time before she comes searching for Kyle. He's ignored answering three calls since I've woken up.

"Where is she?" I say.

"What? Becca? She's in class, I think."

I don't answer which is an answer in itself.

He knows exactly what I'm implying, his crazy girlfriend, her deep-seeded jealousy that keeps her lying in wait, weapon in hand, overnight in a parking lot.

"Tia, yes, she has a restraining order against her, but she, she wouldn't do something like this."

I look up at the tiled ceiling, my heart fast in my chest because I'm about to give myself away, what I found out about her. If pressed, the story will come back to me using his password and getting into her academic records.

"Ask her what she likes to do with tire irons."

"I don't know what the hell you're talking about."

I change the subject because he really does sound confused like he has no clue about the assault and I'm in too much pain to enlighten him. The inside matter in my head feels too large for my skull. I need to get a nurse to give me something strong to make it stop, to numb me into a glorious stupor.

"Why'd they let you in here?"

Kyle shrugs.

"They seem to think I'm your husband because we share the same last name. Who am I to correct them?"

I feel myself smile. I am embarrassed that he's found out I haven't changed back to my maiden name yet. I slip my hand from his. Yet it *is* comforting to have someone here even if it is my ex-husband.

Detective Ramirez parts the curtains while Kyle holds a plastic cup of water with ice chips and a straw to my lips so I may take a drink. In the interview room the detective asked me point blank if I've been having an affair with my ex-husband which I denied. This tender gesture on Kyle's behalf might cinch in the detective's mind I'm clearly lying.

Kyle immediately springs up out of the chair.

"I'll wait down the hall so you two can be alone."

"I've called your fiancé, Catia," the detective says to me, though it sounds more like a fore-warning message for Kyle to do more than linger nearby, but to get out of the hospital before Hugh arrives and there is a confrontation.

Kyle doesn't care about appearances and leans over the bed railing and kisses me on the cheek. Being first at my beside after such a traumatic event means he can get away with it.

"When you feel up to it, meet me at the condo at the marina. You'll be pleasantly surprised by all the work that's been done on it so far."

When he goes, Detective Ramirez sits in the chair my ex had occupied.

"Your fiancé tells me you've been running around all over town on your own."

The other day I wanted him to refer to Hugh as my fiancé. Now it is annoying, almost patron-izing the way he keeps repeating it.

"He said you canceled lunch plans with him at

the last minute today."

I have no idea where the detective is headed or what point he's trying to make.

"I wanted to get the appraisal of the house in Encino over with."

I leave out the part where I felt like I was being followed or where I've been earlier, the two plaintiffs Elise had been forced by the courts to settle up with.

"So Hugh knew you were going to the house in Encino."

I nod. The motion makes me sick to my stomach and I close my eyes again, waiting for the feeling to pass.

"Of course, I told him."

Suddenly I remember the boy on the bike, the odd color of his hands. They were blue.

"There was a boy," I offer. "He was on a bike and darted out right in front of me on the street. His hands had blue spray paint on them."

I open my eyes.

Detective Ramirez looks interested.

"You think somebody hired that boy to spray paint the message on the outside wall of the pool house? My partner, Sharon, is over there now taking photographs."

The thought is overwhelming. It's defeating and brings tears to my eyes.

"What is it, Catia?" the detective asks.

"If that boy was hired, it means people's alibis don't matter. It means the writing I've been analyzing all this time, the Post-It on the mirror in the women's restroom could've been left by a waitress that was paid off. The same thing for the one I found under the wiper of my car. None of it matters. It's all worthless."

"Not necessarily. Did you get a good look at the boy?"

"Not really. I was so shocked I nearly hit him." A boy on a bicycle in an area that is connected seamlessly by one suburb to the next is nothing short of a needle in a haystack. He'd been mobile on a bike. The boy could've come from ten or even twenty miles away, maybe further out.

Detective Ramirez nods, understanding that finding the boy is a lost cause.

"There's another reason why I called your fiancé, Catia."

He looks like he's about to tell me more than he should, news that is going to floor me even though the ground feels like it's already gone. I'm relieved for a brief moment to be lying down in a safe and secure hospital bed.

"I need to question him about his family."

"Ashley, his daughter, is a freshman at Washington State. His late wife, she drowned in the pool. It was an accident. He was at least two hours away when it happened."

"I know. I've read the incident report. It was ruled an accident."

I don't know why Detective Ramirez is doing this to me. I'm in a hospital with a concussion, several stitches, and he feels the need to mess with my head.

"Then what is it?" My voice rises and I'm sure everyone in this oversized room with all the closed curtains hears me. *"What has Hugh done?"*

Detective Ramirez seems unfazed by my voice getting louder or the fact he's about to rupture my world as I know it.

"It's my understanding you worked on the Lucinda Randall murder case quite some time ago. The victim's son, Luther, shot and killed her and dumped the weapon in the L.A. River. He's on death row at San Quentin."

My chest tightens by what I think might be coming next. I feel like I can hardly breathe.

"Yes," I answer him.

I've been dead wrong about the detective. He's been doing a thorough job investigating the people around me and he's found some things I'm not going to want to hear.

"Hugh knows Luther Randall, Catia. He's Hugh's first cousin on his mother's side."

CHAPTER TWENTY-SIX

"YOU CAN'T POSSIBLY think I would hurt you just because I'm related to somebody you once helped put in prison. Someone who *deserves* to be in there."

Hugh is speaking straight to me as if the detective isn't in the room. Shortly after Hugh arrived, the doctor came in and explained they'd like me to stay the night for observation. My room is private with only a single bed, and Detective Ramirez thought it would serve as the perfect place to question my fiancé. He could've suggested Hugh come to the station and be taped in an interview room like I was, but it seems he wants me to hear what Hugh has to say too or maybe he thinks Hugh will reveal more if I'm here.

I look away from Hugh because I have no idea what to say or what to believe. The room is five stories up and outside the window there's the evening rush of cars loading up in the lanes yet still moving at a steady speed.

I'm not sure which hospital I'm at. I recognize nothing and it's disorienting.

"When is the last time you saw your cousin?"

the detective inquires.

This time Hugh looks at him directly. His blue eyes are vicious like he would separate the detective's bones from his flesh if he had the chance. As a teen, Hugh spent his summers in rural Idaho with his paternal grandfather who was an avid hunter of wildlife. Hugh likes to brag he's been taught how to skin an animal quicker than the machines in a slaughterhouse.

"I told you I have *nothing* to do with that side of the family. I haven't seen any of them in years, decades for Christ's sake. What the hell are you checking up on me for? I'm in love with this woman. I would never fucking lay a finger on her."

Detective Ramirez remains calm now that he has Hugh cracking from the pressure of being cornered in this way, in a small stark hospital room with me, his fiancée, here to witness everything. In a way it's worse than being taped in an interview room.

"You must've found out at some point the connection with your family after spending so much time with Mrs. Wilkins."

The sound of Kyle's last name and being reminded it still sounds like I'm legally married to another man shows on Hugh's face. He is furious, though I get the sense he is starting to wise up and realize he's got to stop falling into the detective's trap.

"I put it together well after Tia and I started seeing each other. I didn't bring it up with her because I didn't see the point. My family has always just been my parents who died some time ago, my late wife and my daughter."

I notice he leaves me out which is understandable since he's talking about his past, not his present yet it still stings.

"Have you lied about anything else with Catia?" the detective asks. It's a reckless question, one posed to simply rattle Hugh more than he already is.

Hugh's eyes are on me again, the private matter of his vasectomy and the reversal procedure, and whether he should tell the detective about it before I do.

I hope he sees that I will not embarrass him and he should just stay silent.

This bombshell the detective just dropped has me reeling. I've never thought to check up on Hugh's background. Meeting his daughter that evening on the private yacht had been enough to make me see him as a concerned single father. Am I that easy to deceive? I remember pinpointing that trait in his writing when he'd written his name and phone number down for me and instead of heeding the warning I'd jotted the number down on another scrap of paper and threw out the damning one. Has Hugh been out to hurt me all this time and I never saw it? Do I even know this man I so easily let into my life?

The nurse enters the room and asks them both to leave. Thankfully, visiting hours are over and I need my rest which also means I'll get my privacy to be alone and think.

In the semi-dark, I lie in bed, hearing the sound

of the nurses right outside my half-open door. One of them is worried what kind of mess their new puppy is making at home with no supervision. The others laugh. Normally, under different circumstances, I would've insisted on going home and not staying the night. I hate hospitals. In less than twelve hours I'll be asked to leave and I find myself dreading it.

Am I safer in a home with Hugh in it or should I kick him out? Demand the other key from him and have the locks changed again? The thought of him thinking it wasn't important to tell me about his blood ties with Luther Randall is an ache that isn't going away.

behind you

Those two words the boy on the bike tagged on the wall of the pool house must've meant very little to him except for the extra twenty or fifty in his pocket. To the person that paid him, those two words were precisely meant to terrorize me so that I first experienced a wave of fear and then seconds later felt what should have been a lethal blow.

Detective Ramirez drives me home from the hospital alone, without his partner, Sharon. While I appreciate the gesture I'm also aware he's staying close because I'm a clue to a puzzle he is frustrated he hasn't figured out yet.

When we reach my house, someone has arranged for my Prius to be parked in the gravel drive and Hugh's truck is gone. Hopefully he senses he needs to give me space, that he's the one who's put our relationship at risk with his lies.

Had I known he is related to one of the criminals I helped put in prison, I most likely would've stopped seeing him. Again, I go back to the day at the coffee house with Kyle when he needled me about just how well I know my fiancé. Instead of being a jealous ex-husband with lingering feelings, he might've detected something wasn't right with Hugh and simply been concerned.

The detective goes through the entire house, making sure it's clear before he hands me back my keys. His expression is hard to read. This case has worn him out. He probably should've retired ten pounds and a couple prescriptions for high cholesterol and acid reflux ago.

The pressures from the Davis Family, from the public to solve the case must be unrelenting and now his case has derailed and is hurtling toward a thirty-five-year old appraiser who makes less than sixty grand a year and less than twenty-four hours ago was nearly killed by a blow to the back of the head. His best lead and only witness has still seen nothing. A part of me feels sorry for him.

"Did the interview last night turn up any leads?"

Detective Ramirez lets out a deep sigh as if he can't believe his own bad luck.

"You must remember what it's like when wealthy people like the Davis's *don't listen to authorities* and think dangling a seven figure reward out to the public will solve everything. Makes our job a thousand times harder. We've been flooded with false tips. The press is now at our doorstep demanding to be given updates. I told them to try and be patient and hold off for a few more days. Ms. Davis's wife was having none of it."

I'm shocked to hear Deborah is the one pushing for the two-million-dollar reward and the nationwide interview when it has been Edward who first came up with the smaller amount for the local paper. He also did nearly all of the talking the other night, along with Gia. Deborah barely answered one question.

"You're sure you shouldn't stay with a friend for a couple days? I could wait while you pack a bag."

Jessica is in the Bay area indulging herself, and Laney is a couple hours away by plane. My mother is so far removed in another country that I won't know where to start if she calls or unexpectedly returns home.

"I'm tired," I say. "I just want to lay down and rest."

Detective Ramirez nods, believing me. I'm really about to carefully shower, not allowing any water near my fresh stitches, change clothes and meet somebody who definitely won't be expecting my call.

"I've requested a patrol car to periodically check on your house throughout the day." He says this as he heads out the door as if not only to reassure me but also to reassure himself.

We're both aware I'm still in grave danger.

I've surprised him by showing up in a fluttery dress and heels. It's a clear cloudless day and sailboats make a pattern of white masts filling up with the force from the wind out on the blue water. The sea salt in the air takes me away from the antiseptic smells of the hospital like I thought it might.

I'm not sorry I've come.

In the sunlight Kyle's blue eyes are the color of the ocean. He's wearing a pair of jeans and a button down shirt which means he's either taught a class earlier or he's teaching one after our meeting. I no longer know his schedule.

He's waiting for me in front of the condominium complex where we still jointly own a two-bedroom condo on the third from the top floor – prime real estate with a panoramic view of the Pacific. A little dried mud is on one side of his pricey Italian loafers, an oversight he would normally catch and wipe away with a damp paper towel before ever stepping foot out the front door. It's unlike him not to notice.

Kyle takes my hand and we move into the lobby. He appears more concerned right now than he did yesterday when I was in the emergency room.

"Are you sure you're up for this? I mean, we could do this another time."

"No," I say. "I'd rather be here than laying around at home wondering when I'm about to get attacked again."

As we wait for the elevator, he persists.

"You know, you really should stay with Jessica

for a couple days."

He doesn't mention Hugh which isn't surprising considering they despise each other for no other reason, really, other than their personal connection to me. Yesterday he left the hospital before Hugh arrived so he can't know about the detective questioning him or that Hugh is closely related to a sick murderer who killed his own mother.

Kyle might vaguely remember the case if I bring it up because we'd been newlyweds back then. The stunning news that a son could ruthlessly stand over his mother, watch her sleep, then position her frail fingers around the trigger of the gun and bring her own arm up so that she awakens to that terrifying moment when she shoots herself in the temple. I'd suffered nightmares for weeks. Not long after that case, Kyle convinced me to follow his route of pursuing a career in real estate and I studied to be an appraiser. He didn't want me in any more danger.

"I can take care of myself, Kyle."

Inside the condo the carpet has been replaced with hardwood floor and the baseboards are all taped up, prepared for the painters to start on the walls. One of the walls has a generous bay window overlooking the water.

"As you can see, the kitchen is still torn up," Kyle says, coming up beside me.

I'm not paying any attention to the kitchen, I'm appreciating the stretch of darker, much deeper water that looks, in the distance, as if it's touching the sky.

I feel his hand on the back of my bare neck.

Gently, he rubs it like he used to whenever he noticed my shoulders tense up from stress like they're doing right now. His touch is both familiar and foreign, confusing like the thoughts in my head that swirl making me unsure of my own footing, a symptom of my concussion. My heart pulses in my ears and I feel like I'm about to have an anxiety attack.

I should get out of here before it's too late, shut Kyle out of the elevator before he catches up with me and walk along the beach until my head clears or get in my car and call Laney, confess to her what I was about to do, which is betray my fiancé with my ex-husband.

Kyle's hand slides around my waist, steadying me or getting a handle on me because he can tell I'm about to bolt.

"Do you remember the afternoon we were at the swap meet in Jamaica? It was so humid we could barely breathe and you were so excited going from table to table hunting for handmade items to take back home with us. All I could focus on were the drops of sweat that beaded up on your neck. And I stopped you long enough to kiss them away."

Kyle lifts the neckline of my dress with his finger and moves his mouth on the bare skin exposed.

"Kyle," I plead. My voice is weak and so is my justification for rejecting him. Subconsciously I must've seen this coming. I put on a dress and I'm in heels.

Kyle used to love me in heels. He liked that when I was in them I was taller than him. He used to tease me that I was his own personal supermodel.

He turns and leans with his weight against the frame of the window, then he pulls me to him between his legs. He is not one to waste an opportunity.

He draws his finger slowly up my thigh and his breathing changes.

I brace my hands on his shoulders, confronting the truth I'm not pushing him away. Part of me wants this. I've wanted it since the day I saw him seated at Kerchkoff's when I met him for lunch and I realized he'd moved on with another woman and I had with another man. The distance Kyle and I were creating away from one another was something we could never reclaim. That overwhelming emotion I felt then is what has brought me here, up several flights to this last picturesque ocean front connection the two of us share.

"I'm not on the pill. Hugh and I are…"

Kyle cuts me off with a kiss that is long and deep, two past lovers in intimate rhythm with one another again. He's not going to use protection and when he unzips his pants, pulls aside the crotch of my panties and he enters me, I close my eyes with disgust at my own actions, for the blissful blind hope that this man I once loved might fulfill the one wish that had ruined our marriage.

He will make me pregnant.

Call it nerves or a jittery case of guilt, but I feel

the heat of someone out there, hundreds of feet below on the sidewalk, watching our every move.

Later when I walk through the front door Hugh is in the kitchen making dinner. The pleasing scent of sizzling steaks frying in the skillet.

He is not going to be so easy to drive out of my life. Do I honestly want him to go? I don't know what to believe or if he really loves me. It is possible not to have any relationship with extended family. I hardly ever see mine.

But what about all the questions I've never asked him? What about his late wife? Did she accidentally misjudge the depth of the pool and strike her head on the bottom and drown? Was Hugh really all the way in Santa Barbara? Did the police check the cell phone towers or did they just take him at his word?

Hugh hears me come in and shouts, "Someone from the Davis Family left a message inviting you to the private funeral for Carson Davis. Just close friends and family, tomorrow at 11 a.m. at Hollywood Forever Cemetery."

Hugh rounds the corner, like everything is normal, a dish towel tucked in the waist band of his jeans, then something stops him before he reaches me in the foyer. He glances at my outfit, the heels. If he gets too close, he'll smell the cologne of another man on me. He'll smell sex.

I see it on his rugged features.

He knows.

A few seconds pass between us, a fierce argument that never starts. It's as if Hugh is expecting me to betray him since he's been caught twice now betraying me. Hugh is fair-minded, almost to a fault. It's one of the qualities that has drawn me to him, his ability to see his role in a disagreement – long term partner material I've always thought.

He and I have never been this way with each other, this careful. We each have the capability to blow apart one another's futures with one word, one name, really, the first name of my ex-husband whom I've just slept with.

The quiet only makes it worse.

"Thanks," I say, referring to him relaying the phone message. "I'll play it back later."

"Why don't you go upstairs," Hugh finally says. "Take a shower. Get into something comfortable and come down for dinner. You really need to take it easy."

I nod, grateful he doesn't accuse me of what we both know I've just done.

"Hey," he calls out when I'm halfway up the stairs.

I stop, frozen in place.

He's had a change of heart and he can't let it go.

Regardless of my head injury, we will have a knockdown fight about my ex-husband.

I look down at the man only a couple days before I never dreamt of cheating on, let alone with my ex-husband.

That day in Jordan's office, I felt myself change.

I wasn't sure how it would happen and now I understand I've become as selfish and manipulative as the people who've hurt me. This new woman might not be the one Hugh would've fallen in love with, but in some ways, he is partly responsible for her.

"You need to be more cautious, Tia."

It isn't exactly a threat, though it's definitely a warning. Hugh is suddenly in a rage over everything he's holding back that he wants to say to me but knows he can't. He jabs a finger towards the front door.

"Someone *out there* wants to really hurt you."

CHAPTER TWENTY-SEVEN

THE PRIVATE FUNERAL for Carson Davis is filmed at every angle *outside* of Hollywood Forever's gates by the press. Unlike the vigil, the media is kept at a strict distance. This cemetery has an impressive stretch of green lawn out front where summer concerts are played and a tall white wall runs the perimeter of the property. Movies are screened on it and the public brings chairs, blankets and picnic baskets and enjoys their place on the grass, losing sight of the fact that in short proximity are rows upon rows of grave markers and buried coffins beneath the sloping green lawns.

Only close friends and family are allowed inside the viewing room, the invitations apparently sent out twenty-four hours in advance by phone to secure a small attendance.

His body that had been mysteriously transported to Spain is now reduced to a golden urn of ashes that rests on top of a stark altar that is missing any type of religious markings. Next to it is an enlarged black and white photo taken from a press junket of his first breakout film, a western titled *Decadence.* Carson's face is young, chiseled, his eyes dark and full of the life he can't wait to live. He's wearing a cowboy hat and his smile looks wide and genuine. The resemblance to his son Edward down to the shape of their eyes is apparent, though Edward's eyes are blue like Elise's.

Carson's ashes will be placed in a crypt inside the mausoleum where other famous people are buried and fans will be able to pay their respects and leave flowers. Carson Davis's crypt made of marble will become the newest stop in a popular macabre tour that takes busloads of fans to famous gravesites where they will take selfies in front of their favorites and post them with sad emoji faces on social media.

It is a demeaning end for many celebrities of a bygone era who lived their lives with class and privacy.

The viewing room is decorated in white orchids and red rose arrangements with rows upon rows of black fold-out chairs that are quickly filling up. Carson's second wife, the vocal coach, enters the room with the help of a four-pronged walker and a man around her age, hunched over yet leading her by the elbow, apparently the stronger of the two.

I recognize a couple of legendary male actors, the kind that have stopped making films decades before and live in gated communities to avoid being seen as elderly, needing the help of canes or wheelchairs to get around.

Only in Hollywood is advanced age treated as some kind of humiliation.

Other people in attendance, whom I've never seen before, most likely are screenwriters, producers and behind-the-scenes movie people Carson had worked with over the years. The mood is somber and respectful - mourners chat, catching up with one another, in hushed tones.

I find it somewhat unsettling that the family has decided to bury Carson so fast with Elise missing for hardly one week. It's as if they've already given up hope that she will be found alive.

I spot Edward off to the side, a few feet away, standing with a slight man in his seventies. They are huddled up, yet I recognize the shiftiness in the man's movements. He's decades older, yet he is the same man Carson was speaking to that day of the viewing when he was barking orders about the press.

Edward claps the man on the back and hands him a white envelope with nothing more than a piece of paper inside. He is not the type to pay someone crudely in cash for services rendered in such a public place like at his father's funeral. He'd be a little more subtle about it, maybe set up an account in the person's name in a bank overseas. I wait until the man walks away, to take a seat for the funeral, before I approach Edward.

"I've seen that man before," I say so that Edward knows I'm expecting to hear the truth from him. "The day of your mother's viewing."

Edward doesn't look like I've caught him in anything other than being Carson Davis's dutiful son.

"Dad had what some might see as an elaborate plan in place, Tia. That was just his way. He never wanted to go just like anybody else on their deathbed. His image, no, *his ego,* was much too grand for a death by natural causes. But you must already know that."

Edward heads onto the short-clipped grass and I follow him, slowly passing waist-length high headstones, the engraved names of strangers, nobody famous that I recognize. There is apparently no concern on Edward's part about the funeral starting without him. From now on, as head of the Davis Family, nothing happens unless it's first approved by Edward.

"Three days before my sister vanished, she called me," he tells me. "She told me Dad had gotten worse. His heart was weakening, that the time it was taking for him to die wasn't just killing him, it was killing her. The rest, I could hardly understand. She was crying so hard. You know Elise. *She doesn't cry.*"

I nod, though he isn't looking at me. I can tell he wants to get this conversation over with. For some reason he needs me to know what they've done.

"I offered to fly out. You know, we could make the decision together, if we needed to turn off the machines. I told her she wouldn't have to do it alone. '''I'm not alone', she'd snapped at me and then she hung up."

Edward stops, then surprises me by pulling out a cigarette from a pack in his inside pocket of his jacket. He holds it between his lips, fishes for a matchbook in his pants pocket, lights the cigarette, then takes a long deep drag. I've never seen him smoke a cigarette before, never smelled smoke on his breath or on his clothes. Offspring of the Davis Family are enigmatic creatures. It is in their genes on their father's side to hide from the world who they really are; every day means a new part to play.

"I thought I'd give her a couple days to calm down. Before *I* thought to call her back, she'd gone missing and I'd heard you'd been by to appraise Dad's estate."

"*What happened* to your father, Edward?"

He takes a last long drag off the cigarette before tapping the light out of it on top of a gravestone, then sliding it in his jacket pocket to relight and finish later.

"My sister did nothing but take care of that man for her entire adult life. He was a good father to us, but a demanding one. Elise managed his finances, paid his bills. At a certain point after he and Gia broke up he was like a ghost in his own life. Then when he got sick…had she done it, I wouldn't have blamed her, not for one goddamn second."

When *is* the death of an elderly person on a respirator become murder or a merciful killing? It's a question the state courts all the way to the Supreme Court in Washington D.C. continue to grapple with.

"But you don't think it was Elise."

"Deborah insists something went wrong and he went into cardiac arrest, shortly after you left that day."

"Right before Elise went missing?"

"Deborah claims in the chaos of trying to resuscitate him and call our lawyer to inform him Dad had had a heart attack, she lost track of her own wife."

Of course, it doesn't surprise Edward that Deborah didn't call 911 or the police. To the Davis Family that would be the equivalent of calling the gossip sites and rags directly - inviting the vultures entrance through the foyer so they may swarm and pick into the flesh of the still-warm body of their loved one.

Numerous legendary figures have passed in ways that don't measure up to their lives. Whitney Houston died from an accidental overdose in the bathtub of a hotel in Beverly Hills, hours before a huge pre-awards bash was about to begin. Many macabre people have requested to stay in the room where it happened as a consequence of the heavy news coverage her death received.

Not so long ago a TV actor suffered a stroke on set and was rushed to the hospital where he later died. The media camped out at every entrance and exit of the hospital hoping to get a money shot of the grieving family, maybe a word or two out of one of them, if pressed, *if chased,* all the way to the parking lot or an awaiting car.

As for Carson, the press and public will get no such chance. He and the family have denied them that final moment. The press and public must settle for something far more swashbuckling, the narrative of an expert boater losing critical judgment because of his daughter gone missing. He takes his sailboat out, searching for some sort of rocking calm among the waves, not realizing the increasing slap and tumble of the water that surges starboard. The undercurrent has become monstrous from way down beneath and inevitably overturns his multimillion-dollar craft. The fact there is no actual footage of his body being recovered from the Atlantic does little now to change the story. A few conspiracists may one day soon stir up questions, but they'll all be dismissed for the wack jobs they seemingly are.

Dying with dignity is one matter that's not so easily afforded to wealthy, famous people. I remember that afternoon before Elise's mother's viewing when Carson Davis was talking about distracting the media. His children must've eventually learned all about the sleight of hand, knew who to call. Edward and other family members might've first thought Elise was staging her own disappearance to throw off the press so that they could carry out Carson's final wishes and make it appear he'd died in a boating accident. In the meantime, the press would spend its time chasing a crumb she left behind in the form of a low-heeled, tan suede pump.

"In some way that does make sense," I acknowledge to Edward, referring to Deborah first assuming Elise purposely vanished, and I feel a fleeting sense of hope that she might still be alive out there, on her terms, not in some dirty, ugly space, bound by her assailant, fearing at any moment she's about to be killed.

"Elise has always had a hard time facing things that are beyond her control."

I think back to Edward's suspicions about me over lunch.

"And you thought maybe I knew where she'd gone."

"It wouldn't have been the first time you'd helped Elise out of the kind of circumstances nobody else would dare get involved in."

We are heading back to the funeral. Both of us somberly aware that if I hadn't been the one to help Elise slip away, it is doubtful anybody else has either.

"My sister would appreciate you being here, Tia. She really would."

I glance toward the front row at Deborah – a much better representative of Elise's than me.

"Her wife is here."

"She sure is."

I'm not sure what to make of his comment other than there is clearly no love lost between him and his sister-in-law. It's almost like he wants me to know how much he dislikes her.

"Have the tips turned up anything?" I ask.

"Too much, actually, but there are a couple of strong ones the police are pursuing. The cops still think it's a kidnap for ransom. My father's death meant too much media attention so whoever has my sister backed off and is waiting."

I think of Marcus, Mrs. Keaton and Mrs. Keaton's angry, athletic daughter, the loud scene her mother says she made at the bank after the reverse mortgage papers were lost and the house was foreclosed on. Even with sealed court documents, any of them could be named among the tips. With reward money so high, acquaintances, even friends and family might turn on one another.

"I may not see you again," Edward explains. "The will is being read tomorrow and I really need to head back to my work. Rasila and I, we run a free medical clinic."

Some might call it insensitive for Edward to leave when his sister is still out there, either alive or dead, the possibility of a ransom call not yet ruled out, while I see it for what it is - a form of self-preservation. His family takes too much from him emotionally. It's why he physically separates himself from them by living several thousands of miles away.

I look around the crowded room for the plain, pretty woman Edward was holding hands with the other night after the interview. Rasila must be a doctor or maybe a nurse, generous with her skills as Edward is with his checkbook. That type of aid must get costly and there could be a part of Edward that is eager to receive his share of his father's inheritance.

I don't see the bearded lawyer and trusted old friend, nor do I see Gia either, but I know they're all here somewhere.

Instead of typical organ music, there is someone in the corner playing classical piano music as if this is an expensive restaurant, not a viewing room at a cemetery.

The funeral is about to start.

Edward gives me a long hug, prepared to move on from me soon.

"The cops promise to keep me updated on their progress in finding Elise."

I don't blame Edward for distancing himself both physically and emotionally. Once back in Nepal, he will prepare to get one of the worst phone calls of his life from Detective Ramirez or his partner Sharon with the news his sister has been found dead.

"Is Deborah going to stand in during the reading of the will for your sister?"

Edward shakes his head like what I've just asked him is preposterous.

"No, no. Carl is holding on to my sister's share of Dad's inheritance. It's untouchable unless she is ruled deceased."

"You don't seem to like Deborah very much."

Edward chuckles awkwardly at being put on the spot.

"It shows, huh?"

"A little."

"My sister told me they've been on the skids pretty much ever since they got married. A couple months ago, Elise was about to call it quits and then Deborah got the wild scheme to get pregnant."

I'd hardly call getting pregnant a wild scheme, especially for a woman who is a medical doctor.

So many people like Edward assume a baby is a desperate act that inevitably pushes a couple away from one another. Many times, it draws them closer together. Deborah and Elise could be that kind of couple – two self-absorbed people with a newly shared interest in another person. A child might make Elise a better person. Given the vengeful way she treated Marcus and Mrs. Keaton, two people with whom she barely knew, I can't imagine the kind of heated arguments between Elise and her wife behind closed doors. Maybe Deborah figured a baby in their lives would soften Elise's sharp edges.

"You do get to be an uncle, right?"

This forces a smile out of Edward.

"Right."

He squeezes my hand and when he walks away I think this exchange will probably be the last time I ever see him.

It occurs to me Elise may have stubbornly wanted to keep her father alive, attached to life support indeterminably until one of his organs shut down. This could have gone on for weeks, months, even another year.

Knowing Elise, she wouldn't budge, not for Deborah, her brother or anybody else, no matter how hard they may've tried to convince her to pull the plug. One of her family members could've grown too impatient to keep on waiting, abiding by Elise's directives. I am, after all, only going on Edward's word with what happened.

Would accessing the money and other assets in Carson Davis's will be enough of a motive to take Elise from her own driveway that afternoon? Greed is always enough – it's behind bitter business disputes, divorces, family strife, and murder.

I'm reminded of Hugh's lowlife cousin, Randall, who killed his mother because he had plans on selling her simple home that sat on a quarter acre of high-priced land in Studio City. If he hadn't been caught, he stood to make nearly a million. For somebody out of work, mooching off his mother, that amount would be a fortune.

The thought chills me.

With Elise out of the way so that Carson can finally be buried means someone in this room is getting exactly what he or she wants.

It's only around five o'clock and the sunset is almost gone. As I glance out through the kitchen window, the peaceful old trees that have been here for hundreds of years, well before the cement foundation of my home was ever thought of being laid down, suddenly fill me with fear.

Somebody could be hiding among them, looking in at me.

I could've been killed the other day. The notes meant to scare me, Elise's car up in flames, tricking me into believing my friend might be burning to death in my gravel drive. All of it has been aimed at torturing me, making me read into things that are all false-bottomed.

Nothing is what it seems.

The former handwriting analyst in me failed to take in to account that someone could've paid off people to write the notes and drop them off. At least the two-word message spray painted on the pool house wall is from the hand of a boy on a bicycle.

I am not the type who makes enemies, yet I have six stitches closing up a gash on the back of my scalp.

Why hadn't the blow killed me?

The perpetrator could've easily struck me again to make sure I was dead. Or was I hit on purpose in a place where it would only injure me?

A squad car circled my drive fifteen minutes ago. Another one should come by again within the hour, though it is a cursory inspection. Someone could already be inside here with me, their hand over my mouth and nose, cutting off my airways and the policeman in the squad car would have no idea my life is about to be snuffed out.

The silence in the house is not helping. It reminds me I'm all alone.

I fill a pot with water and place it on the stove to boil pasta. Though I've never been much of a cook, I've watched Hugh enough times to crush a few tomatoes, add olive oil and garlic and make a fresh sauce.

I should call Jessica or Laney and tell them what's happened, that my head wound is sewn up with six stitches yet my life itself is coming apart at the seams. I've inexplicably slept with my ex-husband while being engaged to another man.

Kyle has called three times today and I've let them all go to voicemail.

I could start with going to Jordan's office. Both of them know he'd taken advantage of me when I'd been drunk at the party that night. I've never told them the extent of it, how Jordan had heavily spiked the one drink he made for me or the way he slept on the couch, me waking up in only my shirt with the buttons crooked.

The shame had been too much for me to share with anybody.

I don't tell anyone anything, I realize.

I collect horrible events in my life like my father dying in his sleep and I store the pain away in a place deep inside me that grows wider and wider, creating more emptiness. For so long I've convinced myself that once I have a child growing in my womb it will somehow complete me.

But that won't work either because it's not that I'm not whole.

I am damaged.

I hunch forward against the sink, my pulse quick, trying to slow my breathing.

The phone rings, startling me, and I jump inside.

It's Hugh.

"I wasn't sure if you heard yet. I just saw it on my phone. An arrest has been made in Elise Davis's kidnapping."

Hours earlier I'd sat in the same room as her family members – her brother, her spouse, her young opportunistic stepmother. All of them are too smart to get caught so easily.

"Have they found Elise?"

"No," Hugh says. "But they've found some of her belongings in the place where he kept her. I think they've found her purse. He kept her in a vacant apartment in a building she owns." Hugh sounds stunned. "Unbelievable," he goes on. "The guy must've gotten scared, killed her and moved her body someplace else."

Marcus O'Brien, the man with the bad shoulder who served me coffee at his kitchen table is really the one behind Elise's disappearance? He'd settled his dispute with Elise, he'd taken the money. He's married and said he was sticking around the apartment complex only so he could save up before finding another place to live. It's possible he kept Elise in an abandoned apartment far away from the other remaining tenants, but with his permanent injury he would've needed help, someone physically stronger than himself and I doubt his wife who works full time at a department store is any sort of power lifter.

Not to mention the motive of revenge is weak and I'm not buying it. The man I met the other day showed no signs of ill will towards me, no flicker of surprise or recognition upon seeing my face when he opened his front door.

Who would've tipped off the police?

Jordan.

He's the one who gave me the short list with the two names on it. Finding Elise's abductor, whether she's been killed or rescued alive, is enough to catapult him into the mayor's office. It sickens me to think I've helped him. If I turn on the TV, I bet he'll be holding a press conference, rushing to take credit before his suspect has been properly interrogated.

Hugh breathes heavy into the phone.

"It's over, Tia. You're safe."

I want to believe Hugh, but I don't. If Marcus is responsible for taking Elise, he is not the person who's left me the notes or struck me in the head. He has no reason for wanting to harm me, unless, that is, he has an accomplice.

"When will you be home?" I ask.

Hugh sighs and there's static on his end like he's in a remote place not close to a cell tower.

"I have to tie things up with the Malibu house and then I'll head back. Maybe two hours, tops."

The image of Hugh sleeping with the wealthy divorcee, revenge sex, isn't his style. Most likely he is following up on his employees' work, tightening the hinges on recently installed kitchen cabinets, closely inspecting the grout work in the shower of a bathroom.

After he hangs up, I realize he didn't ask if I want takeout which he usually does considering he's the one who cooks for us.

Quiet once again, I hear a crackle like someone slowly stepping on gravel outside.

My mind leaps to a crazy conclusion. Hugh really does want revenge for what I did to his cousin. He is the one outside, maybe hiding among the trees which would explain the static I heard on his end. It would explain why he so easily dropped questioning me last night where I'd spent the day when he must've suspected I'd been with Kyle.

I hadn't looked on the phone just now to see if Hugh was calling from his own line or if he was using a burner, erasing his tracks.

He is about to stage a break-in or maybe it is his accomplice, Glen.

Glen had seen me drive up just as he was pulling away with the others who'd looked at the Encino house. How simple it could've been for him to circle back and sneak up on me at the pool house.

My heart pounds with the real knowledge I am about to be murdered in my own house. Carefully, I pick up the phone in the kitchen. There is no dial tone.

A scratching sound is now coming from the front door. The brand new lock is being picked.

My cell is in my purse, tossed on Hugh's ugly recliner in the front room. It's too close to the front door for me to grab it, get away from whoever it is breaking in and then locking myself in the upstairs' bedroom to call 911.

Less than five feet behind me is the back door, my only other form of escape. I do not have my car keys on me. I would have to make it down the road to a neighbor's house barefoot. I'd slipped off my flats hours before when I returned from the funeral.

What if the person knows this?

What if there is another person right outside the back door expecting me to run?

Before I have a chance to figure out what to do, the figure is standing in the doorway, black and shapeless.

The glint of her white-blonde hair appears in the waning natural light left in the family room.

I notice the gun she holds at her side.

Becca has broken into my house.

For a moment, there is only the sound of bubbling water swirling in the pot on the stove.

"You need to get the hell out of here, Becca." My voice is unsteady, hardly believable. "Hugh is on his way home any minute."

She points the gun at me.

"I'll take my chances."

"What do you want?"

She steps closer into the kitchen. Under the track lighting, I see her precise black liquid eye liner is smeared at the corners. She's been crying. Her red lipstick has worn off and leaves a messy pink stain around her mouth and the black cotton dress she has on is stretched out like she keeps pulling at it.

She's been falling apart for some time, since at least her stint at the University of New Mexico. Instead of getting the help she needs, she's relocated to a new state, a new university to attend and fixated on a new lover, Kyle. It's the same old Becca, this time prepared to do irreparable harm, so instead of a tire iron she's come with a gun.

Becca tilts her head to one side as if trying to figure something out. Her eyes are bloodshot and vacant.

"Tell me, Tia. You're the appraiser. What do you think I'm worth?"

I have no idea where she's going with this.

"Becca," I begin.

"No," she interrupts, rattled at her own high-pitched sound she makes.

The gun wavers in her hand and I worry about her right index finger, how it's on the trigger. She certainly isn't thinking straight and could easily press down and let it go off at any time.

"I asked you what you think I'm worth? Do you think I'm worth more than you and your thirty-five-year- old barren womb?"

Her words are cruel, breathtakingly so, and though I'm at a loss at coming up with a response, it doesn't appear like she's won anything. She only looks more visibly distraught.

"Or maybe you *are* pregnant, you fucking slut."

Her eyes are pained, the gold color in them gone. Her pupils shrunk down to two black beads, and I think she might be on something. There will be no talking her down. She will do whatever it is she's come here to do and get away with it.

"I watched you yesterday fucking Kyle at the condo. *I saw the expression on your face.*"

I shudder inside at the thought of her watching Kyle and me having sex. She had to have been standing hundreds of feet below on the sidewalk looking up with binoculars.

Suddenly Becca grabs the butcher knife off the counter I'd used to chop tomatoes with. She is ambidextrous, the type who can expertly use both hands. She could've written all of the notes. She either wants to keep me from having something to defend myself with or she wants to use the knife on me. Maybe shooting me dead, she realizes, would prove too easy. I need to suffer more.

"Do you know what *he* told me when I agreed to help him scare the holy fuck out of you? *He* said he was just trying to get you back."

She laughs. It's full of mirth, pure poison.

"Now I see the joke was on me. He knew it too. Professor Wilkins is always so goddamn clever. He really was *trying to get you back*."

Becca lifts the hem of her skirt and cuts her thigh with the knife, a shallow jab, not deep enough for stitches, yet it's going to bleed. Scabs the size of shell bugs cover her entire thigh, a destructive pattern of self-loathing.

Becca is no longer necessarily the type to at first strike out. She now has perpetuated the need to hurt others onto herself.

I can't decide whether she will shoot me point blank from where she stands or if she'll lunge at me with the butcher knife.

Either way I am defenseless. Then I'm reminded of the boiling water on the stove a few feet away from me. My hands will burn without using pot holders, but if I can hold on long enough and aim right, I might save my life.

Becca sets the knife on the counter next to her. A trail of blood leaks down her leg, pooling in her grimy white Converse shoe. It's as if she's numb to the pain. She pulls out her cell phone from a pocket in her dress and presses a number.

She waits a couple seconds before speaking.

"What...is she with you?"

She.

Elise.

Becca has called Kyle and he has Elise. She must be alive.

They've moved her from wherever they'd been keeping her. How would the two of them know to plant her things at the apartment complex?

The court documents had been sealed. Only Elise and Marcus knew the connection between them. Kyle said he never knew Elise, meeting her briefly only that time at our wedding reception when she gave us the weekend hotel stay. With everything that's happened in the last few minutes, anything is possible now.

Becca smiles at me childlike without showing any teeth, then puts her finger to her lips like she and I are somehow in on this together. I think of the education administration classes she's enrolled in, this deranged woman who's gone from one university to the next, unable to ever make up her mind what she wants to do with her life because her focus becomes bent on someone else, the one person whom she decides will love her in the way she demands to be loved and will make sense out of the madness in her head. This woman, armed with both a knife and a gun, is close to earning the proper degree to not only work with kids but also get them alone in her office and mete out their punishment.

"Guess who I'm with," she singsongs to Kyle.

I sense with alarm she's about to kill me.

He says something that makes her expression change.

The gun is pointed square at my chest again.

"You want me to kill her now? Do you want to stay on the line so you can hear the gun shot? No, no, no," Becca shouts into the phone. "Fuck you and your lies. You used me. *Everybody uses me.*"

My eyes move to the pot on the stove, the water rolling in on itself from the intense heat.

Becca catches me. Our eyes meet.

"Your wife here is thinking she can beat me to a pot of boiling water and pour it all over me."

Kyle's voice rises, the words inaudible, though he sounds desperate.

Becca is anticipating my every move and I will not get away. She has had time to concentrate on this moment, to visualize it over and over again, to trap me in my own house.

She must know the layout well from Kyle, from stalking me, leaving the note under my front doormat, driving Elise's SUV here, igniting it in my drive, Kyle waiting in another car nearby. All she'd have to do to go unseen is to make her way through the trees, slip in between a couple homes, suddenly a block or two away, home free.

"Stick to what?"

Becca fakes bewilderment, her index finger in windy little circles next to the side of her temple as if showing me Kyle is the one who's crazy.

They both fucking are.

I had sex with the man who's been terrorizing me, who struck me in the back of my head and then played my rescuer at my bedside in the emergency room, and I fell for it. I called him up the next morning just as he planned.

In many ways I am my own victim. Other women, smarter women who don't spend so much time second guessing themselves, would've seen this coming.

Becca shakes her head repeatedly, sobbing.

I inch towards the stove. I'm close enough now to grab the pot and hurl it towards her. My hands tremble at the thought of carrying so much weight, withstanding the burns.

Suddenly, Becca quiets down on her own, her mind seemingly made up. She almost looks rational.

She's no longer even looking at me but out the kitchen window. Without the moonlight, the darkness of the trees is somehow only visible when the leaves flutter in the breeze. It seems to have a calming effect on Becca. She turns towards me so she and I are face to face again.

The cell phone is still held up to her ear.

"Listen up, Kyle, 'cause I'm only going to say this once."

In one fluid moment she opens her mouth, shoves the barrel inside, and pulls the trigger.

CHAPTER TWENTY-EIGHT

MARCUS O'BRIEN IS held without bail for three days until someone sightseeing off a cliff in Ventura County notices the shiny bumper of the car between the boulders at the bottom of the beach. It's a patch of road that's frequented often by locals, so drivers rarely stop.

There are skid marks on the road where the Mercedes plunged off the side. That must've been the time when Kyle heard the gun go off and he assumed Becca had shot me. He must've lost all sense of direction and braked hard. By the time he realized what was happening it was too late.

His body is found along with the body of Elise Davis.

Becca hadn't really set out to kill me that evening in my kitchen. But she'd turned desperate. She was tired of being told something she no longer believed to be true. She knew what she saw that day looking up at Kyle and me in the condo in Marina Del Rey. She was testing her lover's feelings for me, his ex-wife, the woman he refused to let go of.

When he failed, and she could hear that failure in his voice, confirming her worst fears that he was only using her to get to me, she knew what she had to do. She abandoned the rest of their plans because she now had nothing to lose. So in that moment when she looked out the window at the leaves moving in the trees, a calmness took over. It steadied her hand, the one that was about to move the barrel into her mouth.

As the two of them held onto the same line that was crackling and continuing to grow with unpredictable tension, she turned Kyle's vulnerability of loving me back at him as if it was the sharp end of a knife plunging right into his chest. She knew her words and the sound of the gunshot would end both their lives for she was not about to allow Kyle to get away with his deceitful plans of leaving her for me. She counted on him being too distraught to drive here to my home to see what he thought would be my dead body. She knew the gruesome image she created would blur his vision, that because of it his vehicle would turn into a deadly weapon.

I think back to that afternoon at Kerchkoff's with Kyle. *I* was the reason why Elise had been taken. It was her connection to me, our past friendship, her immense wealth now. The *couple of opportunities* he was waiting for to pan out had nothing to do with real estate. They had everything to do with the members of the Davis Family and the amount they might fork over for the safe return of Elise, the matriarch of the family. Being around all those moneyed people must've soured him down deep because he'd never be one of them. He'd only be allowed to hock their house or teach their children should they sit in his class. In effect, he was one level above the servants who made the beds or answered the front door. That day in my kitchen I'd heard the sudden venom in his voice when he insulted his very own clients. Something inside him had snapped and they, like Elise, became a financial means to an end.

Kyle wouldn't have been too greedy. He'd ask for a couple million, enough where the family wouldn't balk, instead just retrieve the sum from the bank. Maybe Edward already knew about the ransom demand at the cemetery and was letting me know I could hang onto the hope that Elise was still alive and it was only a matter of time before she was safe again. Saying he was leaving town could've been a ruse to throw me off from asking any more questions.

Apparently, Elise had not been tied up and hidden in the trunk of Kyle's Mercedes. From the looks of the crash, the sheer force of the impact, she oddly appeared to be in the passenger seat beside her kidnapper. That part didn't make sense to me. Had Elise somehow gotten through to Kyle and bargained for her life? Was he bringing her home the night of the deadly car accident, back to Deborah and their unborn baby when Becca drastically altered the course of everything by showing up at my house with the gun? They are questions that can't possibly be answered because, I realize, every person implicated in them are all dead.

After Detective Ramirez releases Marcus, Jordan quickly launches into damage control, the press holding him accountable for the speedy rush to judgment, a black man with no criminal record arrested when it turns out he'd been innocent all along.

Jordan loses a good ten points in the polls and finds himself trailing his opponent by two. The election is in five days.

It's a cleanly solved case – Elise, the victim, is unfortunately dead, the assailants, Kyle and Becca, are dead too. Detective Ramirez and his partner Sharon close the case and refuse to make a comment to the press. Their job is officially done and neither of them are looking for accolades.

The nausea is steady now in the mornings. At first, I attributed it to the effects from the concussion. But then comes an aversion to certain favorite foods, then a missed period.

I take a pregnancy test in the bathroom twice and in minutes both surface as positive.

I do not know if I'm carrying the child of a decent man who I'm still engaged to or if I'm carrying the child of a psychopath. A man who I'd been married to for close to ten years, made weekend home improvements on the house with, playfully flicked our sopping paintbrushes at each other while we covered the entire front porch with a fresh coat of paint. We traveled to warm, palm tree lined places like Jamaica and Miami, to boring ones too like the local grocery store or I'd keep him company while he got his beloved Mercedes serviced at the dealer's, and we used to enjoy sharing endless cups of morning coffee. This man, whose last name is still on my driver's license, I never knew him at all.

My moving on so quickly after our divorce must've eaten away at him.

It made him want me back.

It made him hate me for it.

The thought consumed him until he set a course of events to occur along with a sick young woman who knew all about the depths of obsession.

I can't help but think back to the evening in my mother's kitchen with Laney. She saw something in me I didn't. It was an ominous prediction of my life to follow, a foregone conclusion that I will always prove a poor judge of character. First there was Jordan, then came Kyle.

What Kyle did to me is another form of sexual assault, one where he slowly manipulated my situation, devised a way into my life by making me scared of everyone else around me, but him. Hugh had made things easier by deceiving me, but I still willingly sought Kyle at the Marina Del Rey condo the next day after my injury.

I am a victim of my own bad choices. I'm not sure if I'll ever know how to make good ones.

CHAPTER TWENTY-NINE

HUGH IS HEATING up the grapeseed oil in the iron skillet while I'm chopping the yellow and red bell peppers. He's going to show me how to cook chicken fajitas with Spanish rice made from scratch.

I need to learn how to cook. I need to learn how to do a lot of things, how to pat my newborn's back after feedings until the troublesome bubble of air escapes from that fragile little throat. What to do to avoid diaper rash, colic and worse.

My mother reassures me it will all come naturally, most of it anyway. For the rest she claims she'll be around to help. She called the other day from Madrid and when I told her the news she'd be a grandmother again she let out a genuine cry of elation as if this would be her first grandchild and she didn't already have three up north in Oregon. I left out the part about the baby's paternity being in question. Nobody but me and Hugh know.

We are my baby's parents.

Hopefully I'm breaking the pattern of not doing the right thing by staying with Hugh. He's promised he won't lie to me again and with Kyle gone I think it's a promise he'll now be able to keep.

Regardless of the paternity, he insists he wants to be my baby's father just as we'd planned and plans are what we're hinging everything on until we get our relationship fully back on track.

Hugh slides his hand behind my neck, giving it a gentle rub as he oversees the last of my chopping, a skinned white onion.

I blink back tears from being so close to its strong aroma.

"You're getting all the credit for tonight's meal," he decides. "I'll point out the spices you need, how long to brown the meat and no one will be the wiser."

Five minutes after six I hear Jessica's Lexus on the gravel drive. More than one car door opens and closes. She is talking with someone, her voice animated, alive. Then there is the lower sound of a man's response, a chuckle maybe. When I part the curtains in the front room I see it's a man I've never met before but have heard all about – the guy from San Francisco responsible for the extra pounds around her mid-section and the healthy grin on her face. Jessica has never looked happier.

They are both in sweaters and jeans. He's carrying a vase-worthy bouquet of elegant flowers, she a bottle of Pellegrino sparking water. I haven't told Jessica that I'm in my first trimester, though she's the type of close friend who either respects the fact I'm trying to get pregnant or is very much hoping I already might be and therefore shouldn't have alcohol.

I will tell her at a later date when it's just the two of us, in case curiosity gets the better of her and she peppers me with questions about the timing.

She hasn't seen me in weeks, not since that afternoon I showed up frantic at her office and used her computer. On more than one occasion we've spoken on the phone, her sensing I needed some space to absorb everything that's happened, that a part of me inexplicably feels like a grief-stricken widow even though I'm legally divorced from Kyle. I'm mourning far more than my first marriage. I'm mourning my past that I thought I knew to be true because I lived it yet I have to find a way to accept that most of it was built on a lie. Kyle was never the man I fell in love with or thought him to be.

At the front door, Jessica gives me a long hug, expressing how much she feels for me without having to say the words which, when it comes to our decades-long friendship never come easily for her. Our friendship, strangely enough, only grew stronger after sleeping with the same guy all those years ago in college. We've been brutally honest with one another at all the right times, fiercely supportive when the other is too weak for tough talk or rational advice. Our friendship has lasted longer than the respective romantic relationships the two of us find ourselves in now and that I realize is something I am intensely grateful for.

Hugh and Jessica's boyfriend have enough in common to keep up a conversation – a shared interest in the teams on the National League of baseball, a good-hearted roasting of both me and Jessica, how impossible we can be in our own individual ways.

It's a good evening, one I haven't had in a long time, since Elise's disappearance when I feel an encroaching sense of uneasiness overwhelm me. I catch myself looking towards the front door and see that bloody image of a young woman with half her face taken off. As that image fades out, I see another take its place: a man's lifeless body jammed so hard into the steel wreckage of his car that the jaws of life need to pry him out. They are not real, not anymore, I tell myself again. They are only ghosts.

CHAPTER THIRTY

UNLIKE THE LAST time I was at Deborah and Elise's home and I had to wait as Deborah watched me from the window before finally answering my knock, the front door is wide open, held in place by a rubber stopper. On that day I came uninvited. This time Deborah is expecting me. She left word on my voice mail earlier this week that she wanted me to drop by, there was something of Elise's she thought I should have. I returned her voice mail with one of my own, letting her know I'd be by today.

Judging by the small moving truck parked curbside and a young guy coming towards me carrying a long slender cardboard box, the exact size of a computer screen, it appears Deborah might be making a permanent change in residence.

I step inside the foyer so that the guy can pass by me.

"Excuse me, Miss," the mover says, once he spots me over the rim of the box.

Another older man in his fifties is on the younger guy's heels, carrying an ergonomic swivel chair that prevents back pain while seated at a work desk. Further down the hall I spot Deborah, standing under the track lighting of her stainless steel and black marble kitchen.

She's multi-tasking, talking to someone on an earpiece while holding onto her moody cat, its tail ticking back and forth against her pronounced pregnant belly rhythmically like a furry pendulum. Her stomach seems to have popped out overnight, something I can't wait to have happen to me.

She waves for me to come inside, congenial in her demeanor as if I am her old friend and not her late wife's.

Off to the left, the floor drops a step into an expansive family room. Covering the wood floor is a large Santa Fe style rug that takes up most of the square footage, the L-shaped leather caramel color couch, matching light wood coffee table and entertainment center, with the near wall-size screen are too. A canister made of thick glass sits in the center filled with a tangle of black horse shoes. A multi-colored Indian throw blanket rests, double-folded, on the back of the couch. This room is nothing like the more formal living room and I wonder if Elise and Deborah agreed to each choose to decorate the rooms without any input from the other.

It's a nice idea.

My house is too small and maybe I'm a little too stingy with the space I have to give Hugh the green light to add anything more to the décor than that eye sore recliner of his in the front room.

By the untouched look of things, Deborah is

not going anywhere, just having the office furniture taken out and then I remember – Elise worked from home.

Deborah ends her call as the front door closes, the movers on their way with Elise's possessions, including her computer that must store countless crucial documents from her business and personal investments. It must have incriminating information on there too, records of her low-end pay-offs to people who didn't have the money to fight back.

"They're taking Elise's computer to the probate lawyer's office," she explains, leaving her cat on the counter, something Elise would see as unsanitary and never have tolerated, at least not without a very loud protest. "Her furniture I'm donating to charity." She looks down the hallway as if seeing something different than what I do, a shadowy hallway and an empty room overlooking a leafy weeping willow. She leaves without excusing herself, into the room, apparently to retrieve Elise's item she called me here for. "I'm going to turn her office into a play room for our little boy," she calls out to me.

I smile because *I* hadn't even thought about the gender of my baby, just the word baby, its four-letter substance, is all I can focus on.

"A boy? Congratulations."

Deborah returns with a dated black vinyl photo album, the kind my mother still keeps tangible memories of me, Laney and our late father in, with sticky pages and photographs that have already lost their vibrant color. She prefers them in this condition over keeping them in an impersonal file on her computer desktop, although practical Laney downloaded most of them while Mom was on one of her extended trips and took them home to Oregon with her on a flash drive without her knowledge or consent.

"Elise kept a ton of pictures of the two of you as kids. In the pool, balancing on the edge of the diving board, sharing a slice of watermelon. It's almost like she had a lifetime crush on you."

I hear the resentment in Deborah's voice as she gives me the album. The knuckles of her hand have gone white, bloodless from her grip, yet her expression remains ever pleasant, a stark disconnection that makes her hard to read. I wonder if Elise was ever spooked by this too.

"Don't be too surprised. There are other pictures of you in there too. When you're much older. She kept track of your life in these pages as if she was standing right beside you. There are some when you're in your twenties and your hair is long and some of you the way you look now."

I take Deborah at her word and don't open up the album to see for myself. I don't understand why Elise hadn't tried harder to pursue our friendship again instead of keeping me at arm's length for so many years, following me through the safe distance of a camera lens.

For a moment I remember the adolescent girl with the expressionless face who tuned out her mother for that crucial amount of time as she raged and sobbed, then finally the distraught woman stormed out unevenly reaching her

Range Rover where she got behind the wheel and used it to kill herself and an innocent man. Was it an accident or had Mrs. Davis driven over the line on purpose? Elise made me question myself, that I was the one overreacting at what I'd witnessed even though *I knew* in my gut her mother wouldn't ever be coming back.

At that moment Elise turned manipulative. She turned into a boldfaced liar, the story she'd spun for her father right afterwards, as he consoled her in his arms, about where the two of us were, out on the diving board eating popsicles, well beyond earshot when her mother had taken the car. Later as an adult she cheated an old widow out of her home. She cheated a man on disability.

For once Deborah shows on her face how bothered she is at the memory of her wife's feelings for me. It's almost as if Elise was unfaithful to her by keeping this photo album of another woman, of me, for all of these years. No matter how platonic or passionate Elise's feelings for me may have been, in the end her widow and me are both in the same emotional place, alone in our grief, rutted in the past, with the anticipation of a brand new life on the way.

I thank Deborah for her candor and wish her well as she shows me to the door. All I can think about is getting out of that house, away from this very pregnant woman, who lightly places her hand on the small of my back, a half-hearted gesture of affection between two very different women who both recognize they've somehow survived Elise's smoke and mirrors love.

Part of me wants to make a clean break and toss the photo album in some dumpster belonging to a restaurant or a store that I pass on the way home, though I do nothing of the kind. Instead I file it away in the attic on top of my wedding album with Kyle that I still can't bring myself to permanently get rid of, regardless of the fact he nearly destroyed me.

CHAPTER THIRTY-ONE

THE NEXT MORNING while Hugh is rat-tling around downstairs, trying to be patient, waiting for me to get ready, I turn on the water in the bathroom shower. We're spending the entire day shopping for baby furniture.

I stand under the warm beads, increasing the heat, lathering up while letting the water cascade down my back.

Decorating the nursery together is a big step forward for Hugh and me yet I find myself think-ing back to Deborah ridding an entire room of her wife's personal belongings so soon after her death.

Their relationship was clearly a difficult one. Elise had chosen to keep the fact she'd been mar-ried private, not because she was worried what people might think but probably because she wanted out. Her dying father had been the link that kept the two of them together and that was nearing to an end.

The same mechanized oxygen that pushed through the airways to an eighty-one-year- old man's lungs also maintained a dull pulse between two spouses whose marriage had long since been sacrificed in order to keep an unconscious man who wasn't even aware they were in the same room with him alive. How worn out the two of them must've become from doing whatever it takes to conceal his condition from the rest of the world.

While they were expectant parents, I know only too well that the promise to either have or not have a baby is enough to keep a failing relationship alive. Elise had reached out to me after all those years keeping her own intimate collection of my life in photographs she could physically thumb through in secret. Had she hired a private investigator or did she find pleasure in doing the grunt work of tracking me herself? The answer is as baffling, hardened and enigmatic as the woman herself, a woman who never forgot me yet I realize I'd done as much as I could ever since I was thirteen to try and forget her.

While Elise's life was unfairly cut short, she was no innocent. A grieving widow. A man on disability. She hurt those who got in her way, no matter their disadvantages.

A part of her recognized her role in her mother's deadly head-on that afternoon so many years before, though I don't know if she ever felt any remorse for it. What kind of damaged young girl does that and how well she treats or mistreats her spouse later as an adult is anyone's guess.

Some might say there is a perverse underlying justice in Elise dying in a preventable car crash. In the car that night with Kyle haphazardly speeding over the lines of blind turns, she witnessed for herself the explosive initial emotion of losing someone you love.

After I'm done rinsing off, I slide my wet hand to my flat belly where in another four weeks I'll feel the slight change in my body of the baby growing, in time becoming a beating construct of blood, tissue and bone, inside me.

The two of us, we are already physically inseparable. Giving birth will do little to change that.

"Tia," Hugh calls to me from another part of the house.

Suddenly, his voice fills me with a feeling that I can't identify.

I step out of the shower. Steam clouds the glass, so dense and colorless I can write through it and I do. My hand moves so fast I hardly make a sound.

That feeling, I realize, is panic, it's fear, that my baby might love Hugh more than me. I imagine the three of us will be happy, I'm sure of it. I loved my father too much to ever deny my child from experiencing that relationship too. Chasing after the gurney with the squeaky wheel flashes through my mind, how I couldn't breathe, and the paramedic who stopped me before I saw too much, a face blue with death and cold to the touch. But *no man, no father, no body* is ever going to come between me and the pulsing little miracle growing in my womb. If Hugh wants to remain a part of our family, he'll need to respect his place in it.

Someone analyzing my handwriting right at this moment would see the two words I've come up with are deliberate, each letter self-assured and they're already disappearing.

Regardless of how much Hugh loves me and my unborn baby, I will not let that happen.

I won't.

Acknowledgments

Being a female writer, even after the #MeToo movement, isn't easy, and I'd like to thank Mary Ann Brown for her friendship and unyielding support. Special thanks go to Jennifer Kingsbury, Michelle Seward, Betty Pires, Nichole Gilbert, and Naoko Kato. Without these women having my back, I'm not so sure this book would've made it through to the end.

For taking part in my note-writing experiments, I would like to thank Luis Escobar, Emily Roche, and Andrew Salazar. Added thanks to Andy Brown as well.

I can't leave out Joe Acosta and Martin Lastrapes for navigating computer technology for me.

And, of course, always last but not least, to my husband Jim Brown for putting up with me.

ABOUT THE AUTHOR

Paula Priamos is the author of *Inside V,* the Foreword Indie Gold award winner for Best Suspense Thriller novel and the memoir *The Shyster's Daughter.* Her writing has appeared in *The Los Angeles Times Magazine, The New York Times Magazine, The Washington Post Magazine, Crimewave Magazine,* ZYZZYVA, *Mountain News, Orange County Register* and *The Los Angeles Daily News,* among others. She lives in Lake Arrowhead, California.